A Hex A Day

Which Village, Volume 1

L.C. Mortimer

Published by L.C. Mortimer, 2020.

A HEX A DAY

First edition. October 10, 2020.

Written by L.C. Mortimer.

Also by L.C. Mortimer

Enchanted Academy
The Wolf
The Fairy
The Hook
Enchanted Academy Box Set: The Complete Collection Books
1-4
The Beauty

Which Village
A Hex A Day

Standalone
Swords of Darkness
Just Another Day in the Zombie Apocalypse: Episode 1
The Lost Fallen
Outbreak: A Zombie Novel
Shifter Falls Academy: Year Two

Beyond Rainbows: A Zombie Novel
Blood Rum: A Vampire Story
She Smiles at Midnight
Spunky

A Hex A Day

L.C. Mortimer

L.C. MORTIMER

For fans of Buffy, Charmed, and Hocus Pocus comes a story about second chances and new beginnings.

My mom is dead.

At 34 1/2 years old, this shouldn't bother me nearly as much as it does, especially considering the fact that we haven't spoken in years.

But she's my mom.

And it bothers me.

I make my way to her home as quickly as I can. She lived in a little town in the middle of nowhere, but as soon as I start working my way through her estate - organizing the chaos in her raggedy little cottage, sorting through her financial documents - strange things start to happen.

Suddenly, I wonder if I really knew my mother at all.

Suddenly, I wonder if her death was really an accident.

The town where she lived is full of mystery and chaos, and it doesn't take long for me to realize that my mother's killer is still out there - and that I might be their next victim.

For Bobbi and Carol
Thank you for showing me that age is just a number
And that we all deserve happy endings.

Chapter 1

"Your mother is dead."

The voice on the other end of the phone sounded cold and calm, as though this was the most routine thing that they'd had to do all day. What was worse was that it sounded as though calling me had been inconvenient for them.

"What?" I whispered, pressing my cell phone to the side of my head. I must have heard her wrong. There was no chance that what she was saying was true or real. Maybe she had said, "Your mother has read," or "Your mother's got cred." Like maybe my mother just really loves books now, or maybe she's built an incredible reputation for herself and this person thought I should know.

She couldn't be gone.

A heavy sigh.

"Dead," the voice said again. It was cold, calculating. I could tell this person would rather be anywhere but giving me this call, and that rankled me a lot. I'd lost my mother, apparently. This person could at least be kind to me about it.

"What happened?" I asked, clutching the cell phone to my ear. I didn't want to miss a thing. I hadn't spoken to my mother in years. When I'd married Stanley, I'd left home and we'd traveled the world together. Mom had made it clear how she felt about me marrying someone from "out of town." He'd been a stranger to her, and she'd had no interest in getting to know him, so I'd gone away, and I'd never looked back.

My mom had moved to a little town in the middle of nowhere, and despite the essential breaking up of our relationship, we'd written letters to each other a few times a year.

Correction: I'd written *her* letters.

I sent her postcards from China and notes from Japan. She'd gotten gifts of chocolate from when I'd been in Italy and a tea set from my visit to Vietnam. I'd never forgotten my mother, but I'd also never been able to get in touch with her. The few times I'd tried to call to see if I could visit, she hadn't taken my calls. She'd always texted me later and told me not to visit her. She'd been nasty and mean, and finally, I'd stopped trying.

I never really understood what was so horrible about Stanley that my mother had to hate him. After he'd died, I'd wanted so badly to reach out, but it hadn't really seemed like it was something she would care about.

Besides, what would she do?

It wasn't like she'd ask me to come stay with her.

"An accident," the voice on the other end of the phone said.

"Her death was an accident?"

"Yes."

"Like, a car accident?"

"Something like that," the voice said.

What did *that* mean?

"Okay," I said. "And who are you?"

"I'm her attorney," the woman said. "Eliza Warthog."

Strange name, I thought, wrinkling my nose automatically. No wonder the woman sounded grumpy. I would, too, if I had a name like that.

"Well, I appreciate you calling."

"We can handle the estate without you," she said. "I have a team available who can clean out your mother's property, sell it, and send you a check. You don't even need to come to town."

She spoke so matter-of-factly, as though she expected I wouldn't actually want to see my mom's house. Well, she was entirely wrong. Probably, she'd be disappointed when she found out that I actually *did* have plans: big ones, in fact.

The truth was that I'd been trying to visit for years, and I was curious about my mom. I had nothing going for me anymore. Stanley had just died a few months earlier, and I'd been living in a short-term vacation rental until I figured out what to do. We spent so much time traveling around that we hadn't accumulated many worldly goods. I had two huge backpacks: one for each of us. That was it.

The decision was simple.

"That's not necessary," I said. "I'll come tomorrow."

Silence.

The woman cleared her throat.

"I don't think you understand," she said. "Dealing with a loved one's death can be very, uh, traumatic, especially when it's unexpected."

"Don't you dare sell my mother's stuff," I said, and now I was the one who spoke harshly. "I said that I'll come tomorrow. What are your office hours?"

"Well, I have normal business hours," she said. "Nine-to-five, but-"

"I'll be there to pick up the keys before five."

I ended the call, packed up my stuff, and called the owner of the property to let her know I was going to be checking out early for a family emergency. She was completely understanding, and she even offered to give me a refund on the unused time I'd already paid for, but I told her to keep it. She was thrilled, and she promised to rate me as a 5-star guest on the app I'd used to rent the house.

It took me less than an hour to clear everything I owned out of the house and to put it into the car. When I'd returned to America, I'd gone to CarMax and bought a decent, new-to-me car that I could count on. It was a smaller SUV, but it was bigger than anything I'd ever driven before in my life. Now, I was happy for it because it meant that no matter where my mother's cabin was, I'd be able to access it easily and without any problems at all.

I got in the vehicle and sat there for a moment. Should I be going this readily? This easily? Probably not. My mom hadn't wanted to see me when she was alive, so the chances of her rolling over in her grave at the idea of me coming now were high. Still, I couldn't leave this alone. I hadn't gotten a chance to bury my husband. I wasn't going to lose that ability when it came to my mom. She might have hated me at the end of her life, but once upon a time, my mom had loved me.

I was going to do right by her.

I was going to go take care of her things.

WHICH VILLAGE WAS AN unusual sort of name for an unusual sort of place. I'd never really understood the name of the town or why my mother had chosen to go there. She was a retired schoolteacher, after all: not an artist, or a writer, or a hippie. She was just some lady who had chosen the most random place in the world to make a home.

The village was located in the heart of the mountains. It took me seven hours to get there from the city, and as my SUV made its way deeper and deeper into the mountains, I found myself grateful that I'd stocked up on food and supplies along the way. I had no idea what Which Village had as far as a grocery store went. They likely didn't have many modern conveniences, if any. I knew they had a post office, but beyond that, I wasn't really sure.

It was around three in the morning when I pulled into town. The lawyer had called me after business hours for some reason. Maybe she'd been working late. I had no way of knowing. The little town was located in one of the most beautiful places I'd ever seen. Driving in at night had been stupid. I should have waited until morning, but something about knowing my mom was *gone* had gotten me moving. The roads had been terrible, windy, and annoying.

WHICH VILLAGE was painted on a little sign just outside of the town. Below it: POPULATION 4250.

I felt like that was definitely a stretch. There was no chance there were that many people in this little deserted town. Not by a long shot. They had to be including people who lived in the county and not just the actual town. There was a little gas station, a tiny grocery store, and then, I hit pay dirt.

A motel.

The sign said WHICH VILLAGE INN. There was no indication as to whether or not there was a vacancy, so I pulled into the parking lot and looked at what I was dealing with. Despite the fact that this place was kind of a dump, it had a certain charm to it. There was a main lobby that probably doubled as a home for the owners, as well as three little cabins. So, it seemed as though it wasn't a *motel* so much as it was short-term accommodations, but I'd take what I could get.

I went to the front office, but the door was locked. Apparently, this wasn't the type of place with a 24-hour lobby. I rang the little bell and waited a minute, trying to decide what to do. I was obviously waking up the owners, and I felt a little bad about it. Hopefully, they weren't going to yell at me for showing up in the middle of the night without a reservation. If they didn't let me in, I wasn't sure what I was going to do until morning. Maybe I could just park somewhere and sleep in the car.

I supposed I could go park at my mom's house, as an alternative option, but that seemed like a fast way to have the cops called on me, and it wasn't like I had a key, anyway. Was I really going to break into her home? To me, that felt like a violation. No, I'd figure something out one way or another.

After only two minutes, though, a tiny little pixie of a woman came to the door, peered out, and pulled it open. She looked like a shoemaker's wife. Her white curls were pinned on top of her head under a sleeping cap, and a couple of them were peeking out. Her nightgown was a bright white with pale flowers, and it reminded me a little bit of the grandmothers I'd read about in storybooks.

"Are you lost?" She asked kindly. I kind of got the impression that if I wasn't careful, this was the type of woman who would bake me some cookies and read me a bedtime story. I didn't need to feel cozy or loved. Nope. Not here. I just needed to crash for a few hours before I could go deal with everything that needed to be dealt with. Just a few hours of sleep, and I'd be good to go.

"No," I said carefully. I hoped I sounded normal, and not like I was a total weirdo or a freak. This woman seemed very sweet. I didn't want her to think I was some sort of troublemaker. "I was actually hoping to get a room for the night."

"Oh, is that right?" She said, smiling sweetly. "What brings you to Which Village?"

Her question was innocuous enough, but it wasn't really something I expected to hear while checking into a hotel. I was well aware of the fact that her eyes were on me, and she was watching to see what I was going to say. Was this some sort of test? I didn't really want to give out personal information, but I wanted to get to bed. Honesty might be the best policy.

"Uh," I said. "I'm here because of a death in my family."

"Oh," she said, and suddenly, a sad look crossed her face. "You must be Alicia's daughter. Yes, I thought you might be coming to town. Come on in," she said. "We'll get you a room."

"You knew my mom?" I asked, stepping into the little lobby. I tried to ignore how weird it was that she just *knew* why I was there. Apparently, I really *had* stumbled upon a tiny little village. In the city, nobody knew who you were. Nobody cared about you. Nobody bothered wasting their time wondering why you were coming or going or what you cared about.

It was different here, apparently.

Here, people actually did care.

"Everyone knew Alicia," the woman said. She closed the door behind me, locking it, and then went behind the little counter. The lobby was cute, sparsely furnished, and clean. There was flowered wallpaper on the walls, and I thought I smelled the faint scent of sage.

"I'm glad she made an impression," I said carefully. "I hope it was a good one."

The woman looked up at me sharply, but didn't say anything else. She just started typing on her computer. I was actually a little surprised that she had a computer, considering how tiny and out-of-the-way this place was.

"So, have you had your inn for awhile?" I tried to make conversation as I waited for her to finish typing. I didn't really know what she was doing or what she was up to, but I wasn't really interested in standing in the silence and just staring at her.

"It's been in the family for years," she said, glancing up at me. "My husband and I took over caring for the inn. When we're old and done, our sons can take over."

How quaint. It had been awhile since I'd been around anyone who had a "family business" that they passed down, but I rather liked the idea of it. It was kind of wonderful that this woman and her husband had something they could leave to their kids. It was a sort of legacy, I realized.

"How many rooms do you have?" I asked. I had counted three little cabins. Were there more? Surely the inn couldn't bring in enough money to live off of. Then again, what did I know? Perhaps the cost of living in Which Village was less than what I was used to. Maybe that was why my mom had been able to live here so comfortably.

The woman just shrugged.

"We have enough," she said. "Remind me of your name, dear, so I can log it in my registration book."

She glanced up at me and smiled, baring her pearly white teeth. They were strangely white for an older woman. I understood the woman didn't view herself as old, but I sure did. She was tiny and bent over a little bit, and she had wickedly white hair. I had no idea as to her actual age, and I didn't care. The reality was that she'd lived. She'd lived a lot and experienced a lot. I was a little jealous she'd made it to her age, whatever it was, with her husband by her side. I missed Stanley.

That wasn't why I was there, though, so I pushed those sad, wallowing thoughts aside. If I wasn't careful, I'd spend my entire night thinking about my dead husband and not dealing with my mother's estate. That was the real reason I'd come to Which Village. I just needed to deal with what she left behind.

"Jaden Quartz," I said.

The woman's brow furrowed, and she cocked her head, considering me. I knew what was coming next. She wanted to know why my name didn't match my mother's. After all, there was no wedding ring on my finger. I noticed the woman's casual glance at my hand, and then she asked the question I'd been dreading.

"Not Glaze?"

"Not anymore."

I'd left that name behind when I'd married Stanley. I hadn't really spent too much time thinking about it. In my mind, I wanted to get away from my hometown and my childhood village. I wanted to separate myself from the past and look to the future. That had really been what the name change was all about. Plus, it was something that connected me to Stanley. It was something important that meant the two of us could share more than just dreams.

We could share little bits of ourselves with each other.

I didn't want to tell this woman that, though. That was the kind of information you didn't share with someone the first time you met them. A tragic back story about your dead husband and the truth about why your deceased mother didn't like you? Yeah, that could wait until tomorrow.

Or never.

"Glaze," she repeated, and she looked back down at her computer. She typed, focusing on whatever it was she was doing.

"I didn't catch your name," I said.

"Leslie," she said. She kept typing, and then she looked up at me, and she handed me a key. "You'll be in cabin three," she said.

"Okay," I took the key. It was old, vintage. It looked like the skeleton key you'd find in a horror movie or something like that. "Woah, this is heavy."

"It's not, really," Leslie looked confused and shook her head just a little. "It's actually quite light, especially for an iron key." I got the feeling she thought I was a complete moron.

"Why do you use iron keys?" I asked before I could stop myself. I wasn't trying to be rude. It was actually an honest question.

"To keep the-"

"Leslie!" A deep voice interrupted, and I turned. There was a man standing in the doorway that led, presumably, to their living quarters. "What are you doing?"

"Checking in our guest, dear," Leslie seemed completely unbothered by the man's angry countenance. I looked at him carefully, but said nothing. I didn't really feel like angering the beast, especially in the middle of the night.

"Guest?" He asked, looking me up and down, but I ignored him and turned back to Leslie. "We aren't expecting any guests."

"I know, dear," Leslie said again. She turned to the man and smiled at him. "Alicia's daughter just arrived in town and needs a place to stay."

"Alicia?" Suddenly, the man's tone changed. Did it sound softer? I thought it sounded a little bit softer. Gentler. Had he been friends with my mother? It was a small town.

"Did you know my mother?" I asked.

"Yes," the man said gruffly. He said this firmly, as though there was no other room for any sort of question I might have. He made it quite clear that he didn't want to share more information. Unfortunately for him, I'd inherited my mother's sense of nosiness and lack of social decorum.

"How?" I asked.

"What?"

"How did you know my mom?"

"What do you mean? She lived here."

"Not at the motel," I pointed out. "She lived in town."

"Yes."

"So how did you know her? Were you friends?"

The man's brow furrowed, and he crossed his arms over his chest.

"What's with all of these questions?" He asked.

"I miss my mother," I said honestly. I hoped he didn't feel like I was interrogating him. "I'd like to get to know the people she cared about, at least while I'm in town."

"But you won't be in town long," he said pointedly. "You'll wrap up her affairs, and then you'll go back to where you came from."

I looked at him, but I didn't nod my head or shake it. I didn't give him an answer. Partly, it was because I didn't have one. Was that what I was going to do? Apparently, it was what people expected me to do.

Maybe I wouldn't, though.

Maybe I'd do something else.

Maybe I'd stay.

I was saved from having to answer because Leslie stepped away from her computer and placed her hand on my shoulder.

"Let me show you to your cabin, dear."

Chapter 2

L eslie indicated where I should move my car, so I hopped in and parked it directly outside of the little cabin. The lights were already on inside, somehow. Maybe they were on a timer. I hadn't noticed them on before. The cabin looked rustic, and I felt happy that I'd chosen to stop and sleep in a real bed, even if it was only for a few hours.

The little room itself was cleaner than I could have possibly imagined. In fact, for a place that looked wildly run-down on the outside, it was wildly beautiful on the inside. Leslie didn't seem to notice my awe. If she did, she was probably too tired to deal with it. She helped me with the lock and made sure I could use the key, which seemed a little strange to me, but it was always nice to be over-prepared than under-prepared, right?

Once she left, I looked around the little room. There was a large, four-poster bed in the center of the cabin's single room. To one side was a huge, ornate dresser with a mirror. There was no television set, but there were several other interesting pieces of furniture. Each of them seemed to call me. I'd never been especially interested in furniture at all, but I found myself running my hands over the different tables and stands in the room. There was a bookshelf, but it was empty except for a copy of a random herb guide.

The rest of the room seemed very modern. Maybe it was just dark outside, but the entire motel had appeared very run-down to me. I'd expected to find myself sleeping on a flea-infested bed with paint peeling off the walls, but this place was very different from what I'd thought.

"First impressions aren't everything, I guess," speaking to the silence of the room. I'd brought in only my little overnight bag. It had a change of clothes and my toiletries. Despite the fact that I'd loaded my life's belongings into the car, I had remembered my traveling days well enough to remember to pack a special bag that contained everything I needed for a single night. It had clothes, a book, a hairbrush, makeup...everything.

I went into the bathroom and took a look at the huge waterfall shower and the enormous bathtub that filled the room. The bathroom was almost bigger than my old apartment. How was this possible?

Was the cabin bigger on the inside?

I knew it couldn't possibly be, but I was really shocked at just how pretty everything was. There was no television and no phone, but it didn't matter. I took a long, hot shower, pulled on a t-shirt, charged my phone, and climbed into the big bed for the night. It was soft, like sleeping on a cloud, and I fell asleep and dreamed of my mom.

THE LAW OFFICE OF ELIZA Warthog was located downtown in a beautiful renovated Victorian era home. I wondered what the house had looked like before Eliza took it over because as I stood in front of the building, I couldn't imagine it ever looking any other way. It stretched high into the sky and gave me serious haunted-house vibes. There was a big turret and at least three stories. I couldn't tell if there was a fourth floor or not.

The entire town of Which Village looked different in the daytime, too, but only a little. It was brighter, for one. The buildings were all painted vibrant colors – blue, green, shades of yellow – and everything seemed to be designed to be looked at, stared at. I rather liked it. It was strange, seeing this place. My mother had spent so many years here and I hadn't been around. Part of me felt like I was getting a chance to see a part of her I might never have otherwise gotten to explore.

Now, standing in front of the legal office, I wondered what I was about to walk into. My mother's death had been unexpected and rather strange. Then again, a lot of recent events had been unexpected and strange. For one thing, it seemed as though this town was the kind of town that held secrets. That was probably true of any small, off-the-cuff sort of place, but I had a feeling it was especially true of this particular village.

I was from the city, so I was used to things being a certain way: fast. Even in all of my traveling with Stanley, things had moved very quickly. Our lives had been busy and bustling and wonderful. We'd caught trains and busses. We'd hurried from place to place trying to catch our rides on time. We'd done so many wonderful things, but Which Village was different.

It felt...slow.

I wasn't sure if that was good or bad.

Unfortunately for me, nothing was going to get done if I stood outside of a legal office and just gawked, so I finally got up and started walking up the wide staircase that led to the front door. Then I stared at it.

What was the protocol for this type of situation? It was a place of business, but it was located in an old-looking house. Was I supposed to just barge in? Perhaps the right decision was to knock, but then enter. I couldn't tell.

Suddenly, my mom's voice sounded in my head.

"Any decision is better than no decision."

That was something she'd said to me as a kid. It meant that making a choice, no matter what that choice might be, was important. It meant that no matter what I chose, actually moving forward and making a decision was the only way I could actually do anything with my life.

A lot of people got hung up on problems that didn't really matter. Sometimes you couldn't weigh all of your options endless. Every once in awhile, you just had to jump.

I knocked on the door, and then I entered. I was in a beautiful entryway. There were doors on either side of the entrance. Straight ahead was a hallway coupled with a staircase that led up to the next floor. The staircase was on the right and the hallway was on the left. The staircase had a little chain over it with a sign that said EMPLOYEES ONLY.

Okay, so I wasn't supposed to go wandering up there. Duly noted.

"Hello?" I called out into the space.

Nothing.

No response.

The doors on either side of the entryway seemed closed off for a reason. There was no secretary. There was no one I could check in with. I decided to walk down the hallway, and as I did, I stared at the walls. There were big, beautiful pictures hanging on each side of the hallway. Mostly, there were portraits. The women in them seemed to stare down at me, and I felt the skin at the back of my neck prickle a little bit.

I just wanted to hurry up and get this over with. I didn't want to spend my time loitering around a creepy old house. Surely, dealing with my mom's estate wouldn't take too long. I just had to get over the scary paintings and the weird ambiance in the house.

"Hello?" I called out again. This time, I heard a noise. It wasn't human, though. It was some sort of bird. I reached the end of the hall and to the left, there was an open door that led to a little sitting area. I walked into the room and saw a large black bird sitting in a cage.

I walked up to the cage, ignoring the rest of the space. It was beautifully decorated, to be sure, but I only had eyes for the creature in front of me. It was a lovely raven, and I could tell that whoever owned this bird loved it very much. The cage itself probably cost more than I'd ever made in a month, and the bird seemed calm and serene, almost.

Then it squawked again, and I changed my mind.

"What's wrong?" I asked the bird.

"He's just a crabby old codger," someone said from behind me.

I whirled around, surprised. I was shocked that someone had sneaked up on me. Even though I hadn't been doing anything wrong - I'd only been looking for my mom's attorney - I somehow felt as though I'd been caught red-handed with my paws in the cookie jar.

The woman standing before me had on a suit. Not a suit dress: a suit. It looked like it had been perfectly tailored for her tall, slender body. Her hair was pulled back in a tight bun, but it didn't make her look stern or scary. She didn't look like a professor. She looked every bit the businesswoman, and even though there was a softness around her eyes, I could tell that this was the kind of woman you shouldn't really mess with.

"You must be Jaden," the woman said.

"Yes," I told her. "I'm Jaden Quartz. I'm actually here because I'm supposed to meet someone: Eliza Warthog."

"That would be me," the woman said. She pressed her lips together, but didn't smile. She held out her hand and I took it, shaking it. I was embarrassed that my hands felt a little cold and clammy. Gross. It was just that I was very nervous, and I was completely out of my element.

"It's nice to meet you," I said.

"Likewise, albeit under unfortunate circumstances."

"Agreed."

"Come with me."

She turned and didn't look back to see if I was going to follow. She just started walking down the hall. Of course, I wasn't an idiot. I knew what that meant. She was asserting dominance. She was showing me that she was the one in charge. Great. I didn't care. I just followed her back into the hallway and to one of the doors that were located by the front door.

"I called out when I came in," I said.

"I didn't hear you, dear," she told me, looking over her shoulder as she turned the brass doorknob. "I might have been on a call."

"Okay. I just wanted to let you know because-"

"You didn't want me to think you were snooping?"

"Well, yes."

"I know you weren't snooping."

"Oh, okay."

How had I known this woman all of one minute and she'd already managed to make me feel like I was back in school? Suddenly, I didn't feel like an almost 35-year-old woman. I felt like I was 12.

We went into the office. It looked surprisingly like a normal office. There was nothing creepy in this part of the house. There was a large, simple desk with two chairs in front of it. There were plants throughout the room. Apparently, Eliza liked her greens. There were flowers and a couple of cacti. There was even a miniature tree in one corner.

"This is very nice," I said, gesturing to the space.

"Thank you. I've done my best to make it hospitable. Now, there is the issue of your mother's estate."

Yes.

There it was.

Suddenly, my entire body felt like it was on fire, and not in a good way. Somehow, it hadn't really hit me yet that my mom wasn't just gone. She was dead. She wasn't away on some summer vacation. She wasn't on a wonderful, all-expenses-paid cruise. Nope. She was gone. Perished. Dead. My mom was dead and I had to clean up everything she'd left behind.

I squeezed my eyes shut for a second. Then I opened them and looked at the attorney. She was watching me carefully. She was probably used to people having total breakdowns in her office. Most attorneys were. They were good at dealing with people who were down on their luck and having a hard time.

Why else would you visit an attorney?

If you were meeting with a lawyer, something was wrong. You were either there because you thought you were going to die, so you needed a will, or maybe you were in trouble with the law, so you needed advice. Some people went to attorneys because they wanted a divorce. Some people wanted to have paperwork drawn up for contracts. It was never anything simple, though. It was never easy.

Sitting in an attorney's office felt a lot like sitting in the school office, only instead of waiting for the principal, I was waiting to hear about all of my dead mom's stuff.

Cool.

I took a deep breath, steeling myself.

"Did you and your mother discuss her wishes before she passed?"

"No."

That was an easy enough answer. My mom and I had been someone estranged. Well, no, we'd been totally estranged. There hadn't been any bad blood, though, not really. My mom just wanted to be alone and I always felt the need to respect that. Once I'd left with Stanley, she viewed that as me taking sides. In her mind, I'd made a choice. I'd chosen to run off with a boy, and she didn't really want to be any part of that.

She hadn't been mad, though. Most people might consider our situation and think she'd been mad enough to cut me out of her will and her life, but the truth was that she'd just been resigned to the reality. I wanted to explore, and I wanted to escape. My mom wasn't like that. She always just wanted to stay put. She liked the idea of settling down in one place forever. She wanted to be in a space where everyone knew everyone.

"She left behind a will," Eliza said. She placed a document in front of me. "It basically outlines what she wanted done with all of her belongings."

"And what was that?"

"See for yourself. I'll give you a minute."

Eliza got up and left the room. She left me there staring at the will. It was my mother's final wish, was it? I didn't really want to read it. Somehow, I kind of felt like reading the will meant that I was going to have to actually say goodbye to her, and I just wasn't ready. There were still so many things I had wanted to do with my mom. I'd hoped that I'd be able to visit her and to reconnect with her. I'd thought about it a million times, but the timing had never been quite right.

Besides, I had never been sure how to balance her need for privacy with the fact that I wanted to see her. She would have asked me about Stanley, and if we were still together, and if I'd said yes, that I was still very happily married, she would have been bothered. My mom loved the single life. In her eyes, there was no reason to be tied down to a man. We'd never figured out a way to work around that. Instead, we'd treated each other with absolute and utter silence.

It didn't really seem okay to be going through her last wishes or her belongings without having reconnected with her. All I could think about was the fact that I thought Mom figured I had betrayed her by running away with my husband. Had she missed me, at the end? Had she wondered why I hadn't come to visit her more?

With a sigh, I leaned my head down on the desk. This sucked.

Everything about it sucked.

What did I know about dealing with someone's estate?

You know who was good at this?

My mom.

"I miss you," I whispered out loud.

"I miss you," a soft, feminine voice said. It wasn't Eliza's voice, though, and I bolted upright in the chair.

"Who said that?" I demanded to know.

"Who said that?" The voice repeated. It sounded sultry and smooth, like it had been waiting for someone to notice it. I had the distinct impression that whatever had made the sound was an "it" and not a real person.

I stood up and looked around. It couldn't have been one of the plants, right? Definitely not. There wasn't really anything else in the office, though. There was the desk, a bunch of books on a single bookcase, and the plants.

There were *so many* plants.

"You aren't talking to me, are you?" I looked at the plants, narrowing my eyes. Was I going crazy? This was how it always started, I knew. First, you heard voices in your head. Next, you started imagining things where there weren't any. Finally, you were locked away in an insane asylum. Was that what I was destined for?

"You aren't talking to me, are you?" The voice said again.

Shit.

It *was* the plants.

I jumped to my feet.

"Eliza!" I called out. It wasn't professional like, at all. It wasn't appropriate. I should be addressing her nicely and using whatever the right dialogue was. I stared at the plants.

"Eliza!" One of them called out.

Yeah, they were definitely talking.

Eliza opened the door very calmly and walked in. Her heels clicked against the floor as she walked over to her desk. She completely ignored my outburst and glanced first at the will, and then at me.

"Have you already had a chance to look over things, dear?"

The plants were silent.

I looked over at them, and then I looked back at her.

"Eliza, I have a really weird question for you."

"All right," she said. She sat down and crossed one leg over the other. "What's your question?"

"Uh..."

It was now or never.

I could let her know that I was completely insane, or I could pretend that I hadn't been going crazy. If I let her know I was hearing voices, then she'd probably be legally required to call the hospital or something like that. Maybe she'd even have to have me committed. How did those things work, anyway? I had no idea. I just didn't know anymore.

Maybe it was a sign of weakness, but I decided to play it safe.

"I'm really sorry," I said. "I'm just having a hard time, you know, emotionally." I gestured vaguely around the room. "I didn't expect to lose my mom."

Her eyes softened, and she nodded.

"I completely understand," she said. "Losing a parent is never easy."

"I don't really understand the legal jargon, either," I said. "Is there any chance you can clear a few things up for me?"

"Absolutely," she said.

She reached for the papers and started talking. She ran her finger down the paper as she explained what everything meant. There were a lot of words I didn't understand and a lot of legal terminology that seemed superfluous, but at the end of the meeting, I realized that my mother had left me everything she owned.

Everything.

I walked away from the meeting with my mom's house keys, a copy of the will, and Eliza's business card. She had told me to call her if I never needed her, and I promised that I would. There would still be more paperwork and meetings required, but my mom had put my name on the house when she'd purchased it. I vaguely remembered her doing that. She'd paid cash, so I'd never been required to cosign on a loan or anything like that. She'd made me sign some sort of document, and that had been it. I'd completely forgotten about it until Eliza handed me the keys.

Somehow, I left her office in a total daze. Despite everything that was going on with my mom, I couldn't quite shake the fact that there was something strange going on in Which Village. There was something more than I could understand.

Why did I think the plants had been talking to me?

Why hadn't they spoken near Eliza?

And perhaps most importantly, did this actually mean that I was going crazy?

I got in the car, put all of the documents on the passenger seat, and sat there for a minute. For about the millionth time in the last few months, I wanted to reach for my phone and call Stanley. He'd been my rock forever. He'd always known exactly what to do and how to do it. He'd kept me safe when I hadn't been able to keep myself safe. He'd loved me.

Perhaps most importantly, he'd taken care of me at every turn. I'd never had to feel scared when he was there because Stanley had been the most considerate man to ever walk the Earth.

But he was gone, and so was my mom, so I had to face the rest of this experience alone.

Awesome.

Chapter 3

My mom's house was located at the end of a quiet street. It was obvious that she'd chosen the space that she did because it afforded her a certain amount of privacy.

"Yep, seems like Mom," I muttered. I parked in the driveway of the two-story little cottage. That was what it was, really: a damn cottage. All of the other houses on the road were these massive Victorians with big, towering rooftops, but not my mom's.

She'd chosen the tiniest, coziest little house, and the worst part was that I loved it. I liked it a lot. The design of the house was sweet and simple, and as I grabbed all of the paperwork from Eliza's office and headed up the front door, I couldn't help but notice just how beautiful it was.

This was the place my mom had lived. This was where she'd entertained guests and thrown parties and had her birthdays. When she'd written me letters, she'd written them at this house. How much had she loved this place? Judging by the carefully planned lawn and the row of flowers leading up to the house, I'd say a lot.

And I was struck that I still didn't know how my mom had died.

It was strange, wasn't it? An accident. I'd meant to ask Eliza when I was at her office. I should have. It should have been the first question out of my mouth. I'd forgotten somehow, though. It was strange. When I'd walked into her office, I'd felt wildly uneasy and I'd just...

Well, I'd been really certain that the plants were talking to me.

But I needed to know now.

Before I went any farther, and before I did anything else, I needed an answer to this question.

I stared at the house in front of me, looking at how warm and inviting it was. If I went inside, I was going to get distracted again, and I was going to forget. It was no matter, though. Instead of walking into the house, I reached into my pocket and pulled out my phone. Checking the number on Eliza's business card, I called it. She answered on the first ring.

"Eliza Warthog."

"Hey, it's Jaden Quartz."

"Miss Quartz," she said. "I'm surprised to hear from you so soon. How can I help you?" Her voice sounded crisp and collected. She was all business, all the time.

"I know this is kind of strange," I said. "But I forgot to ask you while we were talking."

"What's your question?" Her voice held a tone that said she didn't have all day and that I needed to get to the point.

"How exactly did my mom die? You didn't mention."

"There was an accident," she sighed. "Which is quite unfortunate, and I'm so very sorry."

There it was again: the same word she'd used the day before.

Accident.

Why didn't I believe that was all there was to it? My mom had been a crazy old bat, but she wasn't exactly accident prone. She definitely wasn't the kind of person who *died* from an accident. My entire life, Mom had been trying to keep me safe in every way. She'd worked her tail off to make sure I was cautious and always prepared.

An accident?

That just didn't seem likely.

"What kind of accident?"

Eliza sighed. I imagined her sitting in her office, surrounded by her weird-ass plants, and spinning a pen around on her desk.

Finally, she seemed to decide something.

"You aren't going to let this go," she said.

"I am not."

"Then it's something I'll need to discuss with you in person."

"Um, should I come back over?" I asked.

"No need. I only have one more appointment today. I'll come by after. You'll be at Alicia's house?"

My mom's house.

"Yeah, I'll be here."

"See you soon."

She ended the call quite abruptly, and I wasn't really sure whether I should be happy I was about to get some answers or horrified that she was going to tell me what really happened. Either way, I needed to hurry up and get inside. The neighbors were definitely small-town busybodies. This was the kind of town where nobody had any privacy, and judging by the neck-high hedges around my mom's yard, I'd say it was a safe bet that my mom was trying to stay out of sight.

Strange.

I walked up to the door, slid the key in the lock, and turned. Instantly, I heard a screech and jumped back as a flash of black fur came flying out of the house.

Was that a cat?

What the hell?

Mom had a cat?

I stared as it ran off, disappearing around a corner. I wasn't going to chase it. Not that cat. That was the type of cat that didn't want to be followed. I'd learned my lesson the hard way on that one when I was nine.

Mom and I had been gardening all day. The house we lived in had a huge backyard, and we'd thought it would be a good idea to plant vegetables back there. It had been a good summer full of snacking on fresh produce, but that particular day was hot and we were both sweaty. I was the one who spotted the little black cat first. Mom had been nervous when she'd seen it. She'd tried to get me to leave it alone. She'd warned me that cats don't like new people, but I hadn't listened.

Instead, I'd found myself moving closer and closer to the little cat. I'd crouched down and held my hand out. It was exactly the way I'd seen other people lure cats, but for some reason, the cat didn't come to me.

"Here kitty," I said. "Come here. Here, here, little kitty."

The cat ignored my calls, and I started to grow impatient. I really wanted to pet it, and I didn't understand why the cat wouldn't come closer.

Finally, I reached out and grabbed it with both hands so I could pull it close and start petting it. The cat had reacted exactly as a cat would, however. It seemed to think I was attacking it or that I was some sort of threat. The feline had screeched, clawing wildly, and cut my arm deeply before I finally released it and let it go.

"Ouch!" I had cried out. "Stupid cat!"

"Now, Jaden," my mother had come over and examined the wound, looking over it as a mother ought to, but she'd been worried about more than my cut. She'd been worried about the cat, too.

"It scratched me."

"That's what cats do, Jaden."

"It didn't have to scratch me," I had started to cry. "I only wanted to pet it."

My mother had consoled me, and she'd hugged me. I'd asked her to promise we'd never get a cat. She'd only sighed as she looked at me. Somehow, I had the feeling that I'd disappointed my mother somehow, but I didn't quite understand why.

After all, it was just a cat. It had only been some silly, mangy thing. I'd wanted to pet it, but that had been it.

My mother helped me bandage the wound, and we'd never spoken of the cat again. I had a long, silvery scar on my arm because of the cat. My mother would sometimes look at it, but she'd never comment about how I had scared the cat, or about how I should have been more careful that day.

Now, as I stared at the place where the black cat had vanished, I wondered what else I hadn't known about my mother.

Had she been a cat owner?

Or that had that simply been hiding in her home since it was now vacant?

Feral cats were known for being clever little things. Was this that sort of situation? Was that cat lost? Maybe it was looking for its forever home.

Turning back to the little house, I stepped inside and reached for the light switch next to the door. It flicked on, and then I was cast into...

Darkness.

"What the hell is wrong with the lights?" I asked out loud. They had turned on for all of half a second, and then they'd shut right back off again. I flicked the switch again, but nothing happened.

All right.

Weird.

Maybe I'd need to flip the breakers. I wasn't sure. Luckily, I had a little flashlight on my key ring, and I pulled it out and flicked it on. I spun the flashlight around, casting light throughout the room.

Mom's house, at first glance, seemed rather neat and tidy. It was orderly, to say the least. There was nothing on the floor. There was no mail piled on the little table in the entryway. It looked like the type of house you would visit, but never live in.

"Nice to see some things never change," I muttered.

I went to the front windows and pulled the curtains open. There was a shade there, too, so I pulled that up. Finally, the house was filled with light, and I could get a good look at everything I was dealing with.

It was adorable.

The living room was painted white and there were white bookshelves with white-covered books. There was a white coffee table with a vase of white roses. They were real flowers, and they'd started to wilt, but it didn't matter. They still looked beautiful.

"Pretty," I murmured, looking around. Could I see myself living in a place like this? My mom had obviously liked it. She hadn't wanted to leave Which Village. She'd stayed for an eternity. Was that what I should do, too?

There was a part of me that didn't think I'd be able to fit in here. Ever. I had traveled the globe and I'd met so many different types of people that a place like Which Village just could never suit me.

Or could it?

I quickly went through the first floor of the house. It seemed simple enough. Once I got all of the windows open, it was easy to see that my mom had spent a lot of time in the little cottage. The first floor had a kitchen, living room, bathroom, and a room that was completely full of books. There was a second floor, and I started going up there with my flashlight held high.

It didn't take long to see that the cottage was basically exactly what I expected. There were two bedrooms upstairs. They were both narrow and small. Attic rooms tended to be on the tiny side. The ceilings were slanted, as though they had been an afterthought in the design of the house. I didn't mind too much. One of the bedrooms was obviously my mother's. Her bed frame was white. The mattress was covered with a white duvet and, surprisingly or not, topped with white throw pillows.

Since when did Mom like white so much?

The other room was some sort of craft room. It was full of bookshelves and boxes and all sorts of chaos. There was a big table at one end of the room with something on it that looked like a cauldron. Okay, so maybe Mom was getting ready for Halloween a bit early. Cool. There was a little bed in one corner that looked like a sort of guest cot. I figured I could sleep there, at least for tonight. Crashing in my mom's bed felt kind of weird and a little invasive.

Logically, I knew she was gone, but it still felt wrong. We hadn't talked in forever. If she was looking down on me and watching over me,

Satisfied that the house was in relatively good shape, I decided to go figure out what was wrong with the lights. There had to be a circuit breaker in the basement. There had been a door in the kitchen that I hadn't explored, so I headed downstairs and pulled it open. Sure enough, there was a set of creepy-looking stairs leading down.

Was I about to be murdered?

Who knew?

I thought about sending a text to a friend with a warning. Something that said, "Hey, if I don't message you back in an hour, tell the cops to come look for my body." The problem was that I didn't have any friends. My high school buddies had all gone off and gotten married and had kids and vanished from the face of the Earth. The people I'd met traveling were like me. They moved around from place to place and it was hard to keep in touch.

There was Stanley, but...

I swallowed hard and stared at the blank space ahead of me. I flipped the switch on the wall, but nothing happened. I turned back to the darkness, staring.

Stanley wouldn't have been afraid.

He would have been bold.

That was the thing about him. He had always been so wonderful. He'd done his best to try to keep me going no matter what. Anytime I'd been nervous or afraid, he'd been by my side whispering that I could do it.

"You can do it," I said out loud.

Then I took the first step.

Creak.

Second step.

Creak.

"Damn, Mom," I muttered. "Try fixing your stairs."

I held the flashlight ahead of me, but I couldn't see much. There were some dust particles floating in the air, but that was all I really got. I managed to reach the bottom of the staircase without slipping or falling through a rotten stair, and I got to the breaker box. I didn't really know what I was doing, but I flipped a couple of breaker switches.

And then the lights came on.

They were so bright at first that I shut my eyes, counted to three, and then opened them again. At least it had worked and I didn't have to talk to anyone about rewiring the house or fixing any of the electrical outlets.

The basement was perhaps the only space in my mother's house that felt familiar. It was messy, but the walls weren't painted white and the concrete floor made me feel like I was back in my childhood home with its unfinished basement and dangling ceiling lights. There were a few boxes in one corner with my name on them. There were gardening tools and snow supplies. I saw a set of skis, some shovels, and even a garden hose.

Mom had been a busy lady, it seemed, and she'd collected things. I walked around for a second and examined different things. Mom had always been a bit of a neat-freak, but the basement had always been my zone. As a kid, I'd hidden in our basement and built forts and explored. I'd created imaginary, far-off lands and far-away places.

Now I was being given another chance to hang out in the basement, only this wasn't a place filled with memories for me. This was a place my mother had stored her unwanted belongings. Perhaps this was where she kept things that were better left forgotten.

It wasn't clear whether I'd be in Which Village for a day or a week or longer. I still hadn't made up my mind as to what I was going to do with the house, but one thing was for certain: I didn't want to spend too much time sitting still. If I did, I'd start to go crazy. I was the type of person who always needed to be active and moving around, so I grabbed one of the boxes with my name on it and hauled it up to the living room.

I was surprised to find that an entire hour had passed. How was that possible? I set the box on the living room coffee table, but then I went into the kitchen to see what kind of food Mom had left behind.

I was starving, and I needed to have something to eat. Besides, I'd need to go through everything and make a grocery list. If I was going to be staying long enough to go through her things, I'd need food to eat. I couldn't depend on takeout. I wasn't even sure if Which Village had a lot of restaurants. I hadn't seen any sort of fast food places this morning. Surely there was a diner or something like that.

The cupboards had ordinary fare: soups, stocks, and some noodles. The freezer was completely empty, save for some freezer burn. The inside of the fridge made me gawk a little, though.

"That can't be food," I muttered, looking at an assortment of glass jars on the top shelf. I was getting Halloween spooky vibes. The jars didn't look like they contained blood, but rather, potions. That was insane, but that was what I thought they were. I looked at the labels on each jar. One said "ELEMENT OF DESIRE" and another one said "LOVE SPEAKS." What the hell did that mean?

Ignoring that, I grabbed a bottle of beer from the fridge door. It was a twist off, so I quickly opened it and started chugging. I let the fridge door slam shut, and I went to the living room, sat down, and started drinking. I'd barely finished half of the drink when there was a sound at the door.

It wasn't a knock so much as it was a rustling.

I got up, went to the door, and yanked it open. There was a woman there. She was probably around my age, but she had bright pink hair that hung in two braids, so it was impossible to say. She could have been 19 or she could have been 40.

"Hi," I said, raising an eyebrow, as if to ask what the hell she wanted.

"Hey, I brought Jasper back," she said. She held up the cat that had run by earlier. I stared at it curiously.

"Jasper?"

"Yeah," the woman said. She bounced the cat a little, obviously wanting me to take it, but I only looked at it. She was holding the cat with two hands, and it was obviously uncomfortable and dangling. Finally, I took pity on the little guy and took him.

"Does Jasper live here?" I asked.

The woman's eyes suddenly narrowed.

"Who are you?"

"Who are you?" I asked her back, irritated. My mom was dead and I was having kind of a weird day. I felt that it was okay for me to be slightly nippy with strangers.

Suddenly, realization seemed to dawn on her.

"Oh, you must be Jaden," she said.

"Excuse me?" How did this pink-haired woman know my name?

"Alicia's daughter? That's you, right? I'm Natasha. I live across the street." She held out her hand. I was holding Jasper awkwardly, but I managed to get a hand over to her so we could shake. It was a weird semblance of normalcy, and it made me feel slightly better about the situation I'd found myself in.

"Nice to meet you."

"You too. I wish it was under different circumstances."

"Same."

"Jasper is, well, *was*, Alicia's cat," Natasha said.

"Got it. Mom had a cat."

"You didn't know?"

"About her pet collection? No."

"Oh," Natasha looked at Jasper and patted him on the head. "Well, I think it's safe to say that she loved Jasper a lot. He was always hanging out around the garden when she was outside."

"Cool."

Just another thing I didn't know about my mom. Why did that suddenly bother me so very much?

"Make sure you give him lots of water, and he loves burgers."

"Burgers?" I looked at the cat suspiciously. "What kind of cat likes burgers?"

"Jasper."

"All right," I said. "Well, thanks."

I turned to go back inside, but I felt a hand on my arm. I turned back, and Natasha was still there.

"If you ever need to talk," she offered with a shrug. "I'm just right over there."

She pointed to a big pink house. Like the other ones on the street, it was Victorian style. It had a huge turret and a big, wraparound porch. It had everything anyone could possibly want. If you wanted to live life as a Barbie doll, that was probably a pretty sweet way to go about it.

"Thanks," I said. "I'll keep that in mind."

Natasha finally left, and I went back inside with my mom's cat. Who knew she'd been a cat person? Certainly not me.

"Well, I guess it's just us," I said.

I set the cat down and he took off, obviously scrambling to go explore the house. I went back to the couch and sat down. Then I grabbed the box I'd brought up from the basement and started looking through it.

The first thing I pulled out was a childhood notebook.

"That can go in the trash," I muttered, flipping through it. There wasn't really much there: just some drawings and doodles. I set it aside and grabbed the next item.

It was a snow globe. I shook it, watching the little bits of snow flutter to the ground. There was a little cabin in the background of the globe. I remembered when my mom gave it to me. I played with it a few more times and then that, too, was set aside.

The rest of the box was filled with random childhood stuff. Most of it could be tossed in the garbage. I wasn't one for collecting, but my mom had been, and she'd saved more things than I thought she probably should have.

When the box was empty, I filled it back up with the things I was going to keep. Then I grabbed the other items that I planned to throw away, and I headed into the kitchen to look for the trash can. I tossed them in, and then I looked around. I realized, suddenly, that there was no cat dish here. Shouldn't my mom's cat have a food bowl?

I opened the cupboards, but I didn't see anything. In fact, there was no sign that a cat ever actually lived here. I definitely hadn't seen a litter box or bags of litter as I'd gone through the house. How strange was that? Surely there should have been *some* sign of Jasper's existence, but there wasn't.

I thought back to Eliza's office. I thought back to the talking plants, and I thought about how many weird things I'd seen since I came to Which Village. My mother had secrets, of course, but there was more to her death than people were letting on.

What had my mom been involved in?

Why had she died?

More importantly, perhaps, *how* had she died?

And how could I find out?

I wondered why Natasha had brought Jasper over. I was beginning to think that I was going totally crazy, but I was also beginning to think that my mother didn't actually own a cat. I remembered reading stories as a kid about shapeshifting monsters and things that didn't act the way that they looked.

The cabin I'd stayed in last night had seemed bigger on the inside than on the outside. The plants at Eliza's office had definitely been talking and echoing what I was saying, and now the cat...where had it gone?

I didn't call its name. I was starting to think that it wasn't a real cat at all. At least, it wasn't my mother's cat. Something weird was going on in Which Village, and I wasn't going to be the only one who didn't know what it was. I might be an outsider, but I wasn't an idiot.

Jasper wasn't on the first floor, and the basement door was closed. He had to be upstairs. I moved quietly up the stairs. I walked as silently as I could. I'd learned as a kid to be sneaky, and when I'd gone upstairs earlier, I'd taken note of which stairs squeaked and which ones didn't. When I reached the second floor, I looked toward my mom's bedroom. The door was open and it seemed empty. The other room, though...

Well, the door was closed *over*. It wasn't shut completely. I pushed it open and sure enough, there was a man in the room rummaging around through some of the books and boxes.

"Where is it?" He muttered. "Come on."

I watched him for a minute. He was naked, which was to be expected since a minute ago he'd been a cat.

I *knew* it.

Suddenly justified, I stepped completely in the room and slammed the door shut behind me. The man spun around, staring at me, and immediately shifted back into his cat form.

So he *was* a shapeshifter.

He meowed loudly, purring, and came over to me. He started rubbing himself against my legs.

So that was how it was going to be, huh?

He wanted me to think that I was imagining things and that he really was just a cat. If he was a cat, then why had I just seen him searching in my mom's room for stuff? Why had I just seen him rummaging? I wasn't going crazy. I wasn't.

I also didn't have a way to trap him. Well, not in the bedroom. He was bigger than me, and he'd be able to overpower me easily if I wasn't careful. Besides, there was a big, beautiful window. If he wanted to escape, he'd be able to just jump out of the window.

But there was a bathroom upstairs, and there hadn't been any windows in that room.

"Come on, kitty," I said. "For a second, I thought I was seeing things. You must be thirsty. Let's get you a drink."

I headed into the bathroom.

MEOW, Jasper purred. He came with me, and I turned on the faucet to the sink.

"Oh dear," I said. "There's no bowl here. Hang on, Jasper. I'll be right back." I turned, closing the cat in the bathroom, and stepped into the hallway. My mother's house was old with big, skeleton-looking keys, and the bathroom key was on the outside of the room. I turned the lock and pulled the key out, and then I just stood there.

Meow?

Jasper's meow sounded less like a normal cat noise and more like a question.

"You're locked in," I said. "So why don't you tell me who the hell you are and why you're in my mother's house?"

Silence.

It was quiet for a long minute, and then...

"So that's how it's going to be, huh?"

Chapter 4

It was strange for me to think that just a moment ago, I'd been alone in my mother's house. Now I wasn't with a cat. I wasn't by myself. I was with some strange sort of man-beast and he was locked in the bathroom. I could hear him breathing heavily, and I didn't like the idea that we were trapped in my mom's house. Was he some sort of murderer? Was he responsible for her death?

"Let me out," he said coolly. I couldn't see the man's face, but I could imagine it. I guessed he was glaring at the door. I could practically feel it.

"Tell me what you want," I said. I wasn't about to let this guy out. Not after I'd totally called him out. Not after I'd trapped him. If he wasn't thinking of murdering me before, he definitely was now.

"Strange. You didn't ask me who I am or what I am. You don't even seem to care about that. Most humans care far more about the fact that I'm a shapeshifter than you." I could hear the curiosity in his voice, and I tried to stop myself from completely freaking out.

It was true.

He wasn't human.

He was a shapeshifter.

So they *were* real.

I felt slightly justified by the thought. I had imagined, long ago, that these things might be real. Everyone wanted to believe that humans weren't alone in the universe. Now I knew that was true. I was far less surprised than I thought I should have been. That bothered me a little bit. Shouldn't I have been scared or concerned? Instead, I was irritated, and I felt like I was on the verge of having a nervous breakdown.

I wasn't *scared* of him.

I was about to freak out because I was so mad.

How *dare* he break into my mother's house. How *dare* he think he could slink around in the shadows searching for things. What kind of horrible creature thought it was okay to go through a dead woman's belongings? Hmm? That was what I was really upset about.

"What are you after?" I asked again. I tried to keep my voice level and even. I didn't want him to think I was scared of him, but he also didn't need to know just how angry I was. Anger was something people could use against you. In fact, any strong emotion was something people could use. That was one thing my mother had taught me: don't let people know how you're really feeling. Not unless you can truly trust them.

A pause.

I wondered if he was going to be honest.

Was the man in the bathroom going to tell me what he was doing or what he was after?

"That's a long story. Why don't you let me out? We can brew some tea and have some cookies and talk all about it. I'll tell you everything."

The man's voice was smooth and sultry. I had a feeling he was used to talking his way out of trouble. The truth was that if I could see his face, maybe his words would have been more effective than they were.

As it was, I wasn't particularly in the mood to find a new guy. Stanley's death still pained me. I wasn't sure how long I was supposed to wait before "moving on" after losing a husband, but today didn't seem like the right day. Some smooth-talking shapeshifter cat definitely wasn't something I was particularly interested in.

"Nice try," I snapped, irritated.

"I could tell you everything you want to know."

I waited, not speaking.

"I could tell you all about your mommy dearest," he continued. "I could tell you who she really was. Maybe you want to know *what* she was. Surely you have questions about that."

Well, if Jasper wanted to get my attention, he had certainly figured out a way. He had obviously grasped that my mother was my weakness. Did I want to find out what she was?

I did.

I had so many questions.

But I couldn't let this guy get to me. That was what he wanted. Right? He wanted me to speak up and beg him to tell me who she was. Well, it wasn't going to happen.

Instead, I just stood there, staring at the closed door. I felt something inside of me: something powerful. Anger coursed through my veins, and I wanted to scream at him. I wanted to yell, telling him what a horrible person he was. I wanted to make him pay for what he'd done. I wanted him to suffer.

Wait a minute.

I blinked.

Where had *those* desires come from?

I shook my head, trying to clear my mind. I wasn't a hateful person. Yeah, he was obviously some sort of thief, but making him pay? That wasn't the kind of person I was. I didn't want to *make people pay*. That wasn't who I was.

Apparently, Which Village was having some sort of effect on me, but I wasn't sure that it was a good one. If anything, I was disappointed with the way being here was making me feel.

I didn't answer Jasper.

What would my mother have said if she was here?

Maybe that was the question I should have been asking. Would my mother be the type of person who would let a little shifter cat get under her skin? Would she be comfortable with that? Or would she fight back?

A knock at the door sounded, and the man fell silent. That would be Eliza coming over after work. Apparently, more time had passed than I'd thought. I stood there, staring at the bathroom door. She knocked again, but still, I didn't move. The inside of the bathroom was suddenly silent, and I knew that the shifter had heard the knock, as well.

"Are you going to answer that?" The man said. "Your guest will be waiting."

I knew what he was thinking. He thought it was Natasha - if that was even her real name - coming back to finish what the two of them had started. Was that how their little ploy worked? She dropped him off at someplace and then he just stayed until he'd stolen everything of value?

Forget that.

Then again, maybe she didn't even realize he was a shifter. Perhaps she thought he really was an innocent little kitty. Maybe she figured that he was a harmless sort of cat: the kind of creature that wouldn't hurt a fly.

"Come in," I screamed down the stairs. I didn't dare move away from the door. What if he escaped somehow while my back was turned? "Come in!" I yelled again.

The front door opened. Apparently, I hadn't locked it. Either that or Eliza had a key.

"Jaden?" She called out.

"I'm upstairs."

Her footsteps sounded, and soon Eliza appeared beside me. She saw that my eyes were glued to the door. She looked from the bathroom door to me.

"Jaden, what's going on?" She asked.

"There's a shapeshifting cat in there named Jasper," I said. "A woman called Natasha dropped him off and said it was my mother's cat."

Eliza blinked, looking at me. Was she going to accuse me of being crazy? Was she going to haul me off to the hospital? Telling her all of this was a huge risk, but it was one I felt like I had to take. I had nobody else who could help me. If anyone knew how to get rid of Jasper or how to make him talk, it was going to be Eliza.

She stared at me for a minute. Then, instead of asking me what was wrong with me or whether I was going crazy, she simply shared some information with me.

"Your mother didn't have a cat," Eliza said.

"I'm aware," I said dryly.

"How do you know he's a shapeshifting cat?"

"He was a cat, and now he's a naked man."

We heard a *meow* coming from inside the bathroom. It was followed by scratching sounds. He was pawing at the door, obviously trying to convince Eliza that he should be allowed to come out.

She reached for the doorknob, but noticed the key was gone.

"Key?" She asked, holding her hand out.

"Don't let him out," I said. "I know it sounds crazy, but he's not human."

"Darling, you're in Which Village," she said. "Of course, he's not human. Key."

I handed her the key, and she slid it into the lock. She turned it, shoved the door open, and then held up her hand and murmured something so quietly and fiercely that I couldn't make out the words. Instantly, some sort of invisible bubble shot from her hand and wrapped around the cat, trapping it.

MEOW.

The cat was still standing on the bathroom floor. He wasn't floating or anything like that. Still, it was strange to see it locked in a sort of giant bubble.

I looked over at Eliza. She was staring at the cat.

"So you're a witch."

"Yep."

"And that's a shapeshifter."

"Yep."

"And it's not your first time seeing one."

"Nope."

"Was my mom a witch?"

"Yes."

"Okay."

I started heading down the stairs.

"Where are you going?" Eliza asked.

"I'm going to need another beer."

I went down to the kitchen and opened the fridge. So the stuff on the top shelf actually *was* a set of potions. My mom really was a witch. It made a lot of sense, honestly. Maybe that was why she didn't want me to visit. She had been dealing with weird witch stuff. I cared far less about the fact that my mother was a witch than about the fact that she'd hidden this oh-so-important thing from me.

Why hadn't she trusted me with this information?

Why hadn't I been good enough for her to share this with?

I sipped the beer, doing my best not to chug it. This sucked, honestly. I just wanted a little bit of peace and quiet while I mourned my mom, but now I was dealing with something totally different.

Now I was dealing with the fact that she not only had these huge secrets she was keeping from me, but that she was a paranormal creature, too. Awesome. Did that make me a witch? Was witchiness something that was learned or inherited?

I went back to the bottom of the stairs. Eliza was still up on the second floor with the cat. I didn't know what she was going to do with it, and I was a bit too tired to care. I called upstairs instead of walking up. Somehow, the idea of moving myself upstairs seemed like it would take a ton of energy.

"Hey Eliza?"

"Yes, dear?"

"So my mom was a witch, right?"

"Yes, dear."

"Does that make me a witch?"

"How old are you?"

"Almost 35."

"You'll be one soon," she explained. "You'll get your powers on your 35th birthday. At least, that's when they're supposed to come in."

"Is that when my mom got her powers?"

"Yes."

That explained why she left when she did. It explains why she wanted to be alone. I thought she was just mad I married Stanley. Apparently, she'd been going through her own stuff around the same time. She'd had me as a teenager, so she was still pretty young when I ran off to get married.

Had she known she was a witch? Had she realized that she was going to get these incredible powers? Or had she just turned 35 and then realized hey, I am super powerful and can do all sorts of cool stuff?

I had no idea.

I honestly had no way of knowing.

Eliza walked down the stairs. The cat followed her. Well, "followed" wasn't quite right. It was still trapped in its bubble, so it sort of floated along behind her.

"What are you going to do with it?" I gestured at the feline.

"Whatever I want," she shrugged.

"Are you going to interrogate it?"

"Probably."

"Are you going to torture it?"

Eliza sat down on the couch and looked up at me.

"You don't know anything about witches," she said. It wasn't mean or accusatory. It was just said as a statement, and it was, in fact, completely true.

"Nothing at all."

"Have a seat." She gestured vaguely at the living room. Aside from the sofa and coffee table, there was no other furniture, but I wasn't about to give up a chance to learn more about my mom, so I sat down on the floor, crossed my legs, and looked up at her.

"You and my mother weren't just business associates, were you?"

"You mean was she just my client?"

"Yes."

"No."

"Were you friends?"

She stared at me.

"Lovers?"

She nodded, slightly.

"So you knew her better than anyone else," I pointed out.

"That's it?" She asked. Now it was her turn to be surprised.

"What do you mean?"

"You aren't going to ask me if your mom always liked women, or why she hadn't told you she had a partner?"

"My mother's life was her own," I said carefully. "She had secrets, and I'm certain they were for a good reason."

Eliza looked at me carefully.

"You know, I underestimated you, Jaden. Your mother always told me you were smart, and I always thought she was just saying that because you were her child. Apparently, I was wrong. I apologize."

"Apology accepted. Now, can you fill me in on this?" I motioned to the cat. He was glaring at us.

"Don't worry about him. He can't shift back while he's in the bubble."

"He can't?"

"It's soundproof, too, so there's no way for him to overhear us."

"Interesting."

"Your mother was a witch. She came here because Which Village is a town for paranormals. There are shifters here, and there are a few werewolves. There are witches and wizards and even a couple of ghosts."

"Back up," I said, shaking my head. "What's the difference between shifters and werewolves? Aren't those the same thing?"

"Not remotely. Shifters are born and werewolves are bitten. The other difference is that shifters, like our friend Jasper here, can change back and forth between forms as often as they want."

"But werewolves can't?"

"Werewolves can't control their shifting, no. Not without a special potion, anyway."

I thought about my mother's fridge.

"Was my mom working on a potion for that?"

Eliza nodded.

"Your mother loved being a part of the paranormal community, but werewolves have never really been accepted. She wanted to be part of a world where they were more able to control their abilities."

Something was bothering me. There was something else that Eliza wasn't saying. She and my mother had been lovers. I didn't know how long they'd been together, and I didn't ask. That seemed like private, personal information that was really none of my business. I didn't need to know any of that. What I did need to know was how she had died.

Eliza hadn't mentioned that.

"Eliza, how did she pass?" I asked.

The question hung in the air between us. I watched as Eliza's face seemed to be overcome with emotion. She didn't cry, though. She seemed stoic. While my mom had been very free-spirited and carefree, I got the feeling that Eliza was the opposite. She had been more grounded and put-together. She was an attorney, after all. She was good at keeping her act together.

"She was killed."

The feeling that overcame me then was a mixture between horror, disgust, and understanding. I thought I was going to puke, and I closed my eyes as I tried to calm myself. I gripped my knees, squeezing them.

"What happened?" I asked.

I had to know.

Maybe it was morbid. Maybe it was strange that I wanted to know how my mom had died, but I did. I felt a need to know that was far beyond anything I could really explain.

"Please tell me," I said.

I didn't like putting Eliza on the spot. The truth was that we didn't know each other, but I needed to know what had happened. Why had my mom been killed? And had Jasper done it?

"At least tell me if it was the cat," I said, pointing at him. Jasper might not have been able to hear me, but he could see me, and his ears flattened when I pointed at him.

"It wasn't the cat," she said.

I lowered my hand, and Jasper seemed to relax.

"You're safe...for now," I hissed at him angrily. He might not have been the one who killed my mom, but I didn't like his involvement. Regardless of what he was after, it wasn't anything good. Who the hell sneaked into a dead woman's house, anyway?

"Your mother was a lovable person," Eliza said. "But she had some enemies."

"Who?"

"People who don't believe werewolves have a place in our society."

"I'm guessing there are a lot of people who believe that."

"More than a few," she said.

"So what happened? I know it probably isn't what you wanted to talk about today," I said. "But what happened to my mom?"

"Jaden, first off, come sit on the couch. You aren't a child."

I looked down at how I was sitting. Okay, I could understand how she might think I looked childish. Trying not to be offended, I scurried up and moved to the couch. Eliza looked over at me.

"When I met your mother, it was right after she arrived. She was brand new to town and she wanted my legal advice on a few issues."

"Like buying the house?" I asked, remembering the papers I'd signed.

"Like buying the house. She wanted to make sure it could be in both of your names, and since she'd never purchased a home before, she wanted to make sure everything was done correctly."

"That was nice of you to help her."

"It was my job," she corrected me. "The attraction was instant, and before either one of us realized what was happening, your mother and I were dating."

"Did you live together?"

"No," she shook her head. "Neither one of us wanted that. We loved each other, but we wanted our space."

It was understandable, I thought. A lot of couples rushed to live together, but being apart had its merits. There was something nice about being able to have your own space, and your own room, and your own area where you could just relax without worrying about another person.

"Did you get married?"

"Again, no," she said. "But we were very close, and we enjoyed our time together very much."

The way Eliza spoke about my mother was charming to me. I liked knowing that my mom had found someone who could make her happy. The truth was that I missed my mother so much that it hurt. Knowing she had someone to keep her company when we'd been estranged meant everything.

I thought about Stanley and how much time we'd spent just hanging out, just loving each other. Our time together, while too short, had been perfect. My mom deserved to be happy. I was glad she'd found someone.

"So what happened?"

"She started doing research into hexes and potions. She wanted to find a way to either completely dismiss the curse of the werewolf bite so that victims could return to their own human form permanently, or she wanted to find a way where those cursed could learn to control the bite."

"Who wouldn't want that?" I said. "It sounds really nice. I like that she did that."

"A lot of people. There are people here who think things should be the way they've always been."

"What way is that?"

"Traditional," she said.

Then she snapped her fingers, and the bubble around Jasper evaporated. He was standing on the floor in his cat form. He was sprawled on his belly. Obviously, he hadn't expected to be dropped out of the bubble.

"Change, cat," she said. She reached for a little blanket that was resting on the back of the couch, and she tossed it to him as he changed back into his man form. He wrapped the blanket around himself, growling. "Don't think about running," she said. "You know I'm faster than you."

"I know nothing of the sort," he hissed.

He still kind of sounded like a little cat.

I didn't say anything at first. I was too enthralled by what was happening. What exactly *was* happening?

Eliza was being kind of a total badass, and Jasper just looked totally irritated with both of us.

"You know," he said, looking at me. "If this wasn't for you being so nosy, I would have been fine."

"Don't insult the girl," Eliza said.

It had been a long time since someone called me a girl. The truth was that sometimes I felt much older than I actually was. Losing my husband had taken a lot out of me, but I didn't really want to admit that to anyone, much less Jasper and Eliza. Sometimes I felt like I was all out of life to live. I knew that wasn't true, but...

Well, I missed Stanley.

And I missed my mom.

"Tell me why you're here," Eliza said.

"I need the potion."

"Why?"

"You know why."

"Humor me," Eliza shrugged. "Pretend that I have no idea what you're talking about, cat."

"I have a name, you know."

"You can use your name once you start being truthful," she said. "Bad boys get to be called by their animal names. You're acting like a petulant little kitten, so that's what I'll call you. Kitty."

He glared at her. Jasper seemed to be considering his options. To be honest, I was surprised I'd managed to lock him in the bathroom. It had been truly surprising to me that the little trick I'd played had actually worked.

Now he had fewer options. I wasn't a witch yet. Eliza was, and judging by her skills, she was pretty powerful. Had my mom been that powerful? Obviously, she had. That was how she'd managed to get herself killed. She'd probably finished the potion she'd been working on. Either she'd finished it or someone thought she had. Either way, her work had been dangerous to people who wanted to keep the status quo.

"I'm the kind of person who knows when to take advantage of a good opportunity," Jasper said. "And I received an offer that I didn't feel like turning down."

"Someone wants the potion."

"Someone wants the *recipe*," Jasper corrected.

"And you think it's here?"

He nodded carefully, slowly.

"Who hired you?" Eliza asked, not backing down.

Jasper only shook his head.

"Oh, witch," he said. "You think you're so clever. So smart. You don't even know who's actually behind the death of your beloved. If you can't solve that, how will you be able to figure out who wants the potion?"

To Eliza's credit, she didn't let Jasper's words get under her skin. Instead, she just shrugged and looked at him. I wondered if it was tearing her up inside, having him be such a dick. She was totally focused, though, and that was probably part of what made her such an incredible lawyer. She wasn't allowing his words to bother her.

She wasn't going to be bullied by him.

Eliza opened her mouth, but before she could say anything, there was the sound of glass shattering. A rock came flying through the front window, completely breaking it. I dropped to the ground and so did Eliza. Glass shards went *everywhere*, including in my hair.

When we both sat up, looking around, Jasper was gone.

"What the hell was that?" I asked. I reached for the rock. There wasn't a piece of paper around it with a threat written. There wasn't anything on the rock at all. Then I realized it wasn't actually a rock. It was part of a brick.

Eliza reached for it, examined the thing, and then looked at me.

"Well, shit."

Chapter 5

"What is it?" I stared at the little piece of brick that Eliza was holding.

"A message."

"What do you mean?"

"It's a warning."

"Look, I'm not trying to be either rude or abrupt, but can you clear a few things up for me? Please try to remember that I'm not from your world," I said.

I was starting to feel a little bit overwhelmed. I wasn't a witch. Not yet. If Eliza's earlier words were true, then I didn't have a lot of time before my magical abilities came into play, but as of right now, I was just a normal, everyday girl.

More than that, I was a normal, everyday girl who just wanted to be able to close up my mom's affairs and move on with my life. I wanted normalcy. I wanted simplicity. From the looks of things, my mom's life had been that way. It definitely *looked* like things had been simple.

Eliza's eyes softened, and she nodded.

"I'm sorry," she said. "This can't be easy for you."

"It's really not."

"Your mom was a good person."

"I think so, too."

"She didn't deserve what happened to her."

"Eliza," I asked. "What *did* happen? You honestly still haven't told me."

"She was hexed," Eliza said. "She was supposed to come over and meet me for coffee one morning."

"When?"

"Three days ago."

"So it's only been three days since she died?"

Eliza nodded.

"It took me a little while, but I finally pulled my head out of my ass and got a move on things. I called you, and I started asking questions around town. No one knows anything. Well, either that or nobody's speaking."

"What did you do when you realized something was wrong?"

"Like I said, we had coffee almost every day. She was supposed to come to my place and she didn't show. I called her, but she didn't pick up."

"So you came over."

"Yeah."

"She wasn't here, though."

"She was in the garden," Eliza whispered. "She'd only been dead an hour or so, according to the doctors." She shook her head, and for the first time, Eliza seemed to be overcome with emotion. "If I'd been faster to realize there was a problem, then I could have saved her."

"That's not true," I said. I knew perfectly well that guilt could destroy a person. If left unchecked, most people would be more than happy to accept the blame for all of the bad things that happened in the world. I couldn't let Eliza take the fall for this one.

"Thanks," she said. "But it's true."

"It's not, and we aren't going to argue. Did the police come?"

"Yes," she said. "Even though it's a paranormal town, we still have a police force, albeit a magical one. They couldn't find anything."

"Nothing?"

"Not at all," she said. "There was nothing left behind. There were no clues. There were no potions or weapons or anything. She was just dead, and there was nothing we could do."

I wondered, for a very brief moment, if Eliza could have been the one who killed my mom. The truth was that I didn't know her at all. I didn't even know if she and my mom had actually been a couple. For all I knew, she could have been someone who was after my mom's potions and charms, and she could have been the one who murdered her.

Looking at Eliza's face, though, I knew that it wasn't her. She had the same look on her face that I had on mine when I found out that Stanley was dead.

It was a look of total horror: of complete sadness.

"I miss her," Eliza whispered.

"We'll find out who did this," I swore.

She looked over at me and nodded.

"Thanks," she said. "I appreciate that."

"She was my mom," I reminded Eliza.

"I know the two of you didn't talk, but she loved you very much."

"I know she did," I said.

Sometimes it hadn't felt that way. Our lives had gone in very different directions. My mom had needed space from everything. There was a part of me that had felt for a very long time that she didn't want me. Now I wondered if my mother's absence from my life had been because she wanted me to move on and do my own thing.

Did she worry about me?

Maybe she'd thought that if I knew she was a witch, I wouldn't do my own thing. Perhaps she thought that I would be stuck with her. Maybe she just didn't want me to know. Did she feel like a freak? There were so many things that could have caused our estrangement.

"She wanted to figure things out," Eliza said.

"I get it."

"She missed your dad a lot," she said softly.

"I know."

"She felt like leaving you was the wrong choice," she explained again. "But she was worried that if you knew what she was, you'd be in danger."

"In danger? Why?"

"Your mom never wanted you to feel like you couldn't travel and explore the world."

"What does that have to do with powers?"

"When you come into your powers on your birthday, it'll take you awhile to learn how to control them," Eliza explained. "Your mom planned on telling you next week about who you really are. She figured she could convince you to come here and train before re-releasing you back into the world, so to speak."

"That's kind of messed up."

"There's not a part of this *isn't* messed up," she said.

"So ignoring all the stuff about me and my mom's relationship," I said, not really wanting to talk about it anymore. "What's the deal with the brick?"

"It's from a famous building in town."

"Which building?"

"The library."

"So?"

"So, legend has it that there's magic in the basement of the library."

"And is this a true legend?"

"Your mom thought so. She spent a lot of time there before she died."

"What was she doing there?"

"Research, mostly. There were some archives down there that library patrons could use. She seemed to think she was going to find more information on werewolves there."

"What was with her sudden interest in werewolves?" I asked.

"I have no idea," she told me. I felt like Eliza was telling me the truth. I couldn't really pinpoint why, but it seemed like she was being honest.

"So, what next? Do we go...I don't know, look for clues?"

"Not tonight," she said. "It's late."

"Uh," I looked around. "Do you want to sleep over?"

"Yes," Eliza said easily. "I was planning to invite you to my place, but seeing as how there's been a break-in, I think it's important that we both stay. Two witches are better than one, and we need to guard your mother's research and belongings."

"I'm not a witch."

"You are in your heart," she pointed out. "I'll take the master bedroom."

THE NEXT DAY, ELIZA woke me up early and after a breakfast of eggs and some sort of weird porridge thing she made, we set off for the library. I wasn't really expecting very much, but the Which Village Library was quite lovely. The building was, as promised, made of old brick. It was a three-story building with a pointy top. I wasn't sure if there was an attic or a possible fourth floor, but the building was huge and lovely and a little bit intimidating.

"So everyone here is a paranormal?" I asked as we got out of Eliza's car and headed toward the front.

"Yep. Keep your voice low while we're inside. You never know who - or what - is listening."

We went into the library and Eliza pasted a frown on her face. I understood now that she did that so people wouldn't try to talk to her. She was a busy woman, and while she was well-respected in the community, she was also very private.

The library had a huge staircase in the center of the first floor that led upstairs. I peered up to the second-floor balcony. There were so many different kinds of books that my heart sort of melted a little bit. I was wildly tempted to explore, but we were on a mission, and we needed answers.

Apparently, we needed answers we would find in the basement.

Eliza led me to a section of books that looked like it was hardly used. A quick glance at the titles showed names like *Hexes and Spells for Beginners* and *Once Upon a Curse*. By the time we reached the end of a row of books, I was totally overwhelmed by the feeling of magic in the air.

That was what I'd been feeling since I arrived at Which Village, I realized.

Magic.

It was everywhere.

The air was thick with it, and I was finding that I didn't mind it as much as I probably should have.

"You're taking this well, you know," Eliza said, grabbing a book off a particularly dusty shelf. The bookshelf spun around, carrying us with it. There was a staircase hidden behind the bookcase, and we started walking down the stairs. The bookcase spun back into place, shielding us from the view of any other library patrons who might walk by. There were electric torches on the walls to guide us down the stairs, but the rest of the space seemed very dim.

"What? Finding hidden staircases behind bookcases? I mean, I read a lot of Nancy Drew as a kid, so it doesn't scare me as much as it probably should."

"That's not what I mean. I mean you're dealing with your impending witchdom very well."

"I don't think that's a real word."

She shrugged and continued walking. The staircase was a spiral one, but the brick walls surrounding it meant I couldn't see anything except the stairs directly in front of me. We could have gone down one story or five and I would have no way to tell.

"I wish my mom had told me," I said.

"I wish so, too."

"I'm sure she had her reasons."

"She wanted to protect you."

"I get it, but I'm not a child."

"I know."

We kept walking in silence. It felt nice that Eliza and I were in agreement, at least with this. My mother had been a good woman, but not perfect.

We finally reached the end of the stairs, and we were in a large, empty basement. As promised, the walls down here were brick. There were also several rows of large bookshelves.

"This way," Eliza said. She pulled the brick out of her pocket and started walking.

"Tell me what we're looking for."

"A place with half of a brick missing."

"Do you have any idea who might have thrown it?"

"Someone who wanted to tell us something," she said.

We walked along the walls, circling the books, but didn't see anything for awhile. Finally, just as I was about to give up hope, I spotted a little section of the wall that looked like it was starting to crumble.

"Here!" I said excitedly. I gestured for Eliza to come over, and she did.

"Perfect."

She held the brick piece up, and it was a match.

"I'm still not sure why someone felt it necessary to break the window," I pointed out. Eliza had patched it up easily with just the right spell. I'd been surprised at how quickly she'd been able to fix it up.

"To get your attention."

"My attention? How did anyone even know I was here?"

The only places I'd gone had been the inn and then Eliza's office.

"You talked to the neighbor," she pointed out.

"Natasha said Jasper was my mom's cat. I'm pretty sure she's working with him."

"Or she just saw the cat loitering around a lot and figured he was your mom's."

We'd gone to Natasha's first thing in the morning, but she hadn't answered. I wasn't sure whether that was a good thing or not.

"Besides, you stayed at the inn, didn't you?"

"Yes."

"Lionel and Leslie have hearts of gold, but they're also old busybodies. If you had the idea that you could just waltz into town and blend right in, I'm sorry to say that you were sorely mistaken."

Rankled, I bristled at her comment. Sorely mistaken my foot. I wasn't really sure what she was talking about. Could people in a small town really talk *that* much? It seemed a bit extreme.

Then again, someone had realized I was there, and they'd quite literally tossed us a clue. They'd managed to get my attention, so if that was what they were going for, then it worked.

"Look inside the hole," Eliza said.

I peered in.

"I don't see anything."

She looked at me, narrowing her eyes.

"Try again."

I looked again, but there was still nothing.

"Nope."

"Your powers haven't come in yet," she sighed. "I thought maybe you'd get them a little bit early, but apparently not."

"What would I see if my powers were here?"

"There are fingerprints inside," she said. "They look like a wolf's paw prints, actually."

"You think a werewolf was here?"

"Either that or a shifter."

"Strange."

"Strange indeed," she said.

"Is there a note or anything else?"

"No."

"Then why this brick?" I asked.

Why here? That was the question. There was nothing in the space where the brick was taken, so what was it that the mysterious clue-giver wanted us to see? That was the biggest question I had. Did they want us to be down here for a reason?

"Is there another hidden room?" I asked hopefully.

"I don't think so."

Eliza looked around the room.

"Maybe something in the books?"

"Maybe," I said doubtfully. I was beginning to feel frustrated. There were too many different issues happening at once. We needed to find out who had killed my mom. We needed to find her hidden recipe. Perhaps most of all, we needed to find out who was sending us a message or a clue. Somebody wanted to help us, maybe. Was this how they were going to do it?

Suddenly, I had an idea.

"Wait, give me the stone," I said, gesturing for Eliza to hand it over. She shrugged, but brought it to me. Eliza's delicate hands passed the brick to me. I looked over it carefully. It didn't look like it had been ripped carelessly away from the wall, and it didn't look like it had fallen out, either.

No, this bit of stone looked like it had been carefully carved. I understood that it was a brick, and that sometimes, bricks fell and crumbled. That was a natural part of a brick building aging. Still, there was something else. Something strange.

I looked at the brick, and then, on a whim, I placed it back in the hole where it came from, and I shoved it deep into the spot.

Suddenly, there was a rumbling noise. It was followed by a little portion of the wall sliding open. It revealed a hidden room, and I turned to Eliza, shocked.

"Okay," she shrugged. "So apparently, there is a hidden space."

"Let's go," I motioned for her to follow me inside. I grabbed the brick piece and brought it with me. I wasn't sure whether I would need it or not, but I didn't have any interest in getting stuck downstairs in the library. Not when there where creatures out *there* looking for me. For us.

"All right."

We went into the little room. Once we were inside, I looked around for a button. I didn't want anyone sneaking up on us while we explored and looked around. As soon as I found the interior button that closed the secret door, I hit it. The wall closed shut, and then we were alone.

This must have been my mother's private space.

"She never told me about this place," Eliza said. She sounded a little hurt.

"Me neither," I shrugged.

"I thought we told each other everything."

I looked over at her. Yeah. She was definitely hurt.

"Hey," I reached for her shoulder. "I might not be a witch yet. I might not have my powers or know a lot about this world, but I know one thing."

"What's that?"

"She loved you. A lot, from what I can tell. If she kept this from you, she must have had a reason."

"I hope so."

"I know so."

The room was small and simple. It was just a tiny little room with a big table in the center of it. There were books sprawled out on it, along with a big cauldron.

"It's not hanging over a fire," I rolled my eyes.

"Not all witches use a cauldron," Eliza pointed out. "And they don't need to be over a fire. It's a cauldron: not a cooking pot."

"Same thing, right?"

"No," she glared. "It's not the same thing."

"I'm joking."

"It's not funny."

"Whatever."

Okay, so emotions were running a little high as we looked around the room. I shouldn't have been acting like a crabby teenager, but she didn't need to snap at me, either. I wasn't exactly a fan of finding out that my mom had these big, horrible secrets, either. That didn't make it okay for her to bitch at me.

"So this is where she came to do her research."

"Apparently."

"What are we looking for?"

I stared at the different little potions of herbs.

"There are a lot of different ingredients," I commented. "I don't really know what we're looking for."

Eliza ran her hand over the lids of different jars. She picked up a couple, examining them. I reached for a notebook and flipped through it. There were lots of different notes. Some of them seemed mysterious and like they were written in code. Other notes seemed obvious.

"Anything in there?" She asked.

"Just a bunch of random notes. Looks like there are a few recipes she tried out. She has a couple of entries in here about recipes that didn't work."

"But nothing that did work?"

"Not yet."

I kept skipping around. It was almost like a little diary. Everything was dated starting a few months ago. I flipped forward to some of the more recent entries. Nothing seemed to really stand out, though.

Not until I got to a note where my name was mentioned.

Recipe 34 didn't work on Quartz. Trying less sage this time.

Strange.

What did *that* mean?

Eliza found a box of note cards and flipped through them. As with the journal, nothing really seemed to matter or make sense.

"We should go," she finally said.

Once we were certain that there was nothing left in the room that could either indicate my mother used it or help us find out her recipe, we left the room, made sure it was locked up, and then headed upstairs to the library.

We were walking down one of the rows of books when we heard someone call after us.

"Hey, you! Excuse me! Yes, you two!"

We turned to see a tall, lanky librarian. She was so tall that she looked almost like a spider. She had deep auburn hair that hung down to her waist in loose curls. She was wearing a pencil skirt and a white blouse. I wasn't sure if she could get anymore stereotypical.

"Can I help you?" Eliza asked.

"I was about to ask you the same question," she said. "I saw you go into the basement."

I just looked at her, not really understanding what she wanted.

"I'm so sorry," I said, feigning ignorance. "Were we not allowed to? I've been looking for a book and my dear friend Eliza was helping me out."

The woman scrunched up her nose and shook her head.

"Eliza knows you're allowed down there. It's just that you were down there an awfully long time. Were you able to find what you needed?" Her question was innocent enough, but I understood the real question: who were we? What were we doing? Were we causing trouble?

"No," I shook my head. "We couldn't find what we needed." Eliza turned to me, as if to ask what I was doing. "I'm looking for a book on herbology and sleep problems. Do you have any recommendations?"

The librarian paused for a second, as if taking in what I'd just said, but then her face seemed to light up.

"Why, yes! I have so many! Come with me and I'll make you a list. My name is Patricia, by the way. Patricia Rubies."

I followed her back to the main circulation desk, and Eliza followed reluctantly. Eliza seemed to think I was being totally crazy and insane, but hopefully my wild and random plan would pay off.

"Nice to meet you," I said. "I'm Jaden."

"Now, Jaden, I'm going to give you a list of books you can try," she said. "Hopefully, at least one of them will help you out."

She started typing on her computer, and then she grabbed a piece of parchment and started writing on it. The parchment was kind of old looking, but it was pretty cool, too. She used a feather quill that she dipped in an inkwell to write.

"Thank you so much for helping me," I said. "I would be lost without this. You have a lot of books downstairs."

"Yes, we really do have quite the collection," she said as she wrote.

"You know, it's really cool that the basement collection is located behind a hidden bookshelf," I said.

"It is nice, isn't it? One of our patrons suggested that as a sort of cool, trendy sort of thing to try out. People love it, though. It's not really a secret, but it's a fun little thing."

"Oh, absolutely. Does your basement see a lot of foot traffic?" I asked casually.

"Not too much. We have one patron who really loved spending time down there. Sadly, she passed away last week."

Eliza tensed from behind me. Obviously, the woman didn't recognize her as my mother's lover.

"Oh, I'm sorry to hear that."

"Yes, me too," she said. "She and her friend used to go down there for hours and just study together."

"Her friend?" My ears perked up at that.

"Oh yes. Nice young man. Handsome, too," the woman winked at me. She kept writing down the names of books. Soon she had about ten names.

"We could all use more of those around, huh?" I asked, trying to keep her talking.

A handsome man?

With my mom?

Who was that?

"Oh, yes. They don't make them like this," she said dreamily. "Haven't seen him in a couple of days, but he's here all the time. Well, he was. Now that his friend has passed, I don't know if we'll see him again."

"That's too bad."

"It really is. Here you go, love." She handed me the parchment. "Now, most of these you can find on the second floor, except for that last book. It's on the top floor. Let me know if you need any help, and I'll take you myself."

"Thank you so much," I said politely. "I really appreciate it."

"Anything to help a patron," she said. "Will there be anything else?"

"Actually," I said. "Do you happen to remember the name of the man whose friend died? I'd like to make sure I share my condolences if I see him."

"Hmm," she said, tapping her chin. "It was some sort of rock," she said.

"A rock?"

"Yes, something like Mr. Diamond or Mr. Emerald...something like that."

Suddenly, my blood ran cold. I thought of the notebook we'd found, and of my mother's notes. I thought of how she'd written a note about me, but what if it hadn't been about me at all? What if the note had referred to someone I shared a name with? Someone else who had been dead?

"Quartz?" I whispered. My mouth was dry, and the word was hard to get out.

"Why, yes!" She grinned readily. "How did you know?"

Chapter 6

"What was that all about?" Eliza looked at me curiously once we were in the car. "You look like you've seen a ghost."

"I think that I have."

"Explain," her eyes narrowed, and she glared at me. In that moment, I was instantly reminded of my mother. That look was one she'd given me many times before: mostly when I didn't think that I deserved it.

Eliza was beautiful. She had very sharp features, but her eyes were completely delicate. It was no wonder that my mother had loved her.

"I was married."

"I know."

"My husband died."

Eliza stared at me.

"When?"

"Recently. Six months ago. My mother didn't tell you?"

"No."

"I'm not sure if she knew."

I had written to her, but I'd never gotten a response. I hadn't really expected one, to be honest. That was the way my mom had been for a long time. She responded when she felt like it, and when it was convenient for her.

"How could she not know?" Eliza whispered.

"I don't know."

"What does your husband's death have to do with the library?"

I stared at Eliza, waiting for her to put the pieces together. I didn't quite understand it myself, but it had to be him.

"Quartz," she finally said. "That's your last name."

"That was my husband's name, too."

"I thought you said he was dead."

"Maybe he's less dead than I thought."

It didn't make much sense to me, though. Had Stanley faked his own death? Had he pretended to be dead, and then come to Which Village? Why would he come here? More importantly, why would he tell my mother that he was alive, but not me?

It hurt. For a minute, I felt like I might throw up.

"Not in my car," Eliza said, noticing my face. "If you have to vomit, tell me and I'll pull over."

"I'll be okay."

"You'd better be."

She drove, pulling out of the library parking lot and heading back to the house where my mother had lived. We heard sirens as we approached. Before we saw the house, I knew exactly what we were in for. There was smoke billowing from that general direction, and people were standing in their yards as we drove closer.

Why was it that bad or dangerous events always attracted a crowd? It seemed like without fail, anytime something bad or horrible happened, people wanted to gather around and just gawk. Apparently, Which Village was just like any other place, except for the fact that a few of the people watching had horns. One person had tiny little wings that looked like they should be in a cartoon about fairies. Another had a big, black robe on. Overall, this was the first time I'd seen the citizens looking less than human. Usually, I felt like everyone was very concerned with appearing "normal."

We drove as close as we could, but thanks to the fire department, the police cars, and the crowds, we couldn't drive directly to the house.

"Someone torched it," I murmured, taking it all in.

"Shit," Eliza said.

We parked down the road and then walked over to the house. Somehow, the short journey seemed to take a million years. The property was swarming with professionals: cops, firefighters, and a few official-looking people who seemed like they were used to being in charge.

"Excuse me?" Eliza said to a woman who had her back to us. She had a long dress on. "What's going on?"

"Eliza?" The woman turned, frowning at us. "What are you doing here?"

"Helena, you know why I'm here." Eliza stared at the woman, who was simultaneously trying to figure out who I was and why Eliza had shown up.

"Hello," the woman said to me. "I don't believe we've met. I'm Helena Porridge."

"That's an interesting name," I said, shaking her hand. "Jaden Quartz."

"I think you win the prize for interesting names."

"Thanks, I guess." I jerked my head toward the house. "That's my house."

"That's Alicia's house."

"Yeah, and mine. We owned it together," I said. "What happened?"

Helena was obviously the person in charge. I wasn't quite sure how. She was tall, though. She kind of towered over both Eliza and me. The softness of her skin made it impossible to tell how old she was. I was getting that vibe a lot from this place. Was she 30 or was she 75? I had literally no way to know. She wasn't the first person I'd met who seemed ageless.

I made a mental note to ask Eliza about that later. Would I be able to acquire this ability to look young forever? No wonder people liked witches so much.

"Helena is the mayor," Eliza said, explaining to me who she was. I appreciated that she didn't wait and make me ask.

"Okay."

"And the leader of a coven," she added.

"Eliza!" Helena screeched.

Eliza only shrugged.

"She's Alicia's daughter. She was going to figure it out sooner or later."

Helena only sighed and shook her head.

"Privacy seems to mean nothing to some people," she muttered.

"Please," I said, trying to diffuse the argument that seemed to be brewing. Apparently, these two had a history, and it wasn't pretty. "What happened?"

"Nobody saw anything," she said. "It was called in by a neighbor."

She gestured vaguely toward a woman with pink braids. My eyes narrowed, and I started marching over to Natasha before anyone could say anything else. Natasha was standing and speaking with a police officer. She had her arms crossed protectively over her chest, and she was holding none other than Jasper.

"Oh, Jaden!" She said when she saw me. She scurried over. "I found Jasper in my yard this morning. He seemed so scared." She held him out, but I glared at Jasper.

"Get lost, cat," I said.

Jasper got down and scurried away. Natasha only looked surprised.

"What was that all about?" She asked as Jasper ran off.

"You don't want to know. That's not my mom's cat, either."

"It's not? But he's always in her yard!"

So, it was just a misunderstanding, was it? I still wasn't completely sure whether I should buy it or not. Natasha definitely *seemed* like the kind of person who was innocent, but that didn't mean much. A lot of people seemed like they were things other than what they were. For example, my mother seemed like she was a human and not a witch. My husband seemed like he was dead and not secretly alive. Lots of people could play tricks on their loved ones.

"Natasha, I need to ask you something."

"Okay?"

"Are you and that shapeshifter trying to rob my mother?"

"What?" Natasha squeaked out. She burst into tears and shook her head. "No!" She didn't ask me who the shapeshifter was.

"You don't need to cry," I pointed out the obvious. "You just need to answer the question."

"I don't even know you," she said. "Why would I tell you anything?"

Eliza and Helena appeared: one on either side of me. They looked at Natasha, and then at me, and then back to Natasha.

"She had the cat," I pointed out. Suddenly, I felt a lot less like an almost-35-year-old woman and more like a 10-year-old girl who was snitching on the little kid across the street. How childish did I seem right now?

That bothered me a little bit, but what bothered me even more was the fact that neither Helena nor Eliza looked alarmed.

"Natasha," Eliza said. "You've lived across from Alicia a long time."

"Yes," Natasha said. "And it's nice to see you again, Miss Eliza. My condolences for your loss," she whispered.

"It's fine," she said tightly.

We all knew that it wasn't fine. I knew more than anyone else here just how *not* fine losing your partner actually was. Few things in life were as horrible and unforgiving as having someone you adored pass away. It sucked. Badly. The thought that Stanley might secretly be alive didn't take away the pain I felt from his loss. For one thing, I didn't know if I could believe it, and I didn't want to get my hopes up that he might be somewhere, lurking around. It still scared me that he might have faked his own death, but not told me.

"We need to talk," Helena said.

"I don't have anything to say," Natasha crossed her arms over her chest and glared directly at me.

Eliza started mumbling under her breath, and Natasha's mouth suddenly closed tightly. I realized immediately that Eliza had put some sort of spell on her, and suddenly, Natasha couldn't speak at all! She shook her head as she tried to speak, but no words came out.

"Bring her into the house," Helena said, glancing around to make sure nobody else had noticed. "I'll meet you there shortly."

She turned back to the firefighters and other emergency technicians who were trying to get the fire under control. Eliza gestured for me to stay with Helena while she carefully guided Natasha back to the pink house across the street.

"So you're Alicia's daughter," Helena said, looking at the workers.

"Yes."

"And you came to town after her death."

"Yes."

"To sort out her affairs, is that right?"

"Yes."

She turned to me and looked me up and down. I had the feeling that Helena was used to having people pay attention to her. She had an air of importance about her. Probably, she liked feeling like the most valuable and intelligent person in any room she walked into. I understood why.

"What's your beef with Natasha?" She wanted to know. Apparently, it had been quite obvious that I wasn't pleased to see my mother's neighbor at the crime scene.

"Do you know her?" She probably did. If Helena was the mayor, then she probably knew more about the people of Which Village than anyone could possibly believe. That could be a good thing, or it could be horrible. I didn't know Helena, so I really had no idea as to whether she was a good person or a bad person or somewhere in-between.

"She's a good witch."

"That must count for something," I said. I couldn't quite get a read on Helena. She was clever, to be sure. She was definitely a very powerful person. I had a feeling that as the mayor and coven leader, she probably knew everything that went on in Which Village: who came, who left. She was the type of person who was used to getting her way. Was she the type of person who got angry when someone crossed her?

"It does," she said. "So, what do you think happened to the house?" She turned back toward my mother's cottage. It was going up in flames, and I was sad about that. It was disappointing, but not for the reasons she probably thought.

There had been so much of my mother in that house. I'd wanted to go through her things. I'd wanted to see what there was to learn about her. So far, all I'd discovered was that my mom had a penchant for potions, and that she'd been working on a cure for werewolves.

If her recipe had been in the house, it was long gone by now. I had a feeling that my mother was cleverer that that, though. If the recipe was anywhere, it was in the notebook I'd pulled from the library basement. Well, either that, or Stanley had it.

If he was actually alive.

He'd always been a sneaky bastard, but I'd never had thought he would be the type of person to fake his own death. What other explanation was there, though? Who else could my mom have been talking about?

Quartz was a type of rock, okay, but her note hadn't made it seem like she was talking about that. Besides, why would she have capitalized the "Q" if she was writing about rocks and not about my husband? I was almost certain she was working on something with him: something they didn't want me to know about.

"I should be asking you the same question," I said to Helena. "You're the one in charge here."

"True," she said, nodding. "And what I think is that it's quite suspicious you come to town and the house burns down the next day." She shrugged, glancing over at me. She seemed to think it was some sort of "gotcha" moment, as though my arrival meant I was the one who burned down my mother's home.

Instantly, I disliked Helena. Maybe it was a witch's intuition, but I suddenly had the distinct feeling that she and my mother had *not* been friends. I made a mental note to ask Eliza about that later. Helena seemed like kind of a busybody, and she seemed like kind of a know-it-all, too.

"Technically, I came into town two days ago," I pointed out, irritated. I choked my anger down, though. I didn't want her to know her comment had rubbed me the wrong way.

"That doesn't exactly convince me of your innocence."

I shrugged. I didn't come to play games. I didn't really care whether Helena Porridge liked me or not. She had a dumb name, and she was kind of crabby. She was also wildly suspicious, but of the wrong person.

"I'm not here to impress you," I told her. "I'm here for my mom."

"Then why didn't you come while she was alive?" Helena asked sharply. "Why are you just now showing up? Call me crazy, but it seems quite strange that you show up and then this happens." She waved her hand in the direction of the fire, and I turned and walked away.

I'd heard enough.

It sucked that I hadn't come and seen my mother sooner. It sucked even more that I was about to come into my witchly powers and didn't have anyone to guide me. Oh, I supposed that Eliza would probably help me out, but it wasn't really going to be the same.

Was it?

I missed my mother dearly, and I regretted that I hadn't been a good daughter to her. It made me feel a little sick to know that she had been alone at the end, and that I hadn't been there for her.

Had Stanley?

That thought kept bugging me, nudging at the back of my mind. Why did Mom say the person with her was called Quartz? Mom and Stanley were both very careful when it came to revealing their identities to people. Even when he was alive - if he was actually dead - Stanley had always been careful when it came to sharing personal information.

It was strange. Had she used his name on purpose as a sort of clue? Had she known that someone might try to kill her?

I marched across the street to Natasha's house, and I opened the door without knocking. I went inside, ignoring the fact that the house was perfectly decorated or that it smelled like cookies. Of <u>course</u> it smelled like cookies. Why wouldn't her house smell perfect?

Eliza and Natasha were in the kitchen, and Natasha still looked like she couldn't speak. Eliza was just sitting there.

"What are you going to do to her?" I asked.

"Wait for Helena," Eliza shrugged.

"Why are you going to wait?"

"She's the coven leader."

"That doesn't mean she's a good person," I pointed out. Natasha's eyes got wide. Interesting. So, she didn't like me insulting her leader.

Eliza just shook her head.

"You have a lot to learn about the politics of being a witch."

"Did my mother have a lot to learn, too?" I asked. That was what I really wanted to know. Had Mom upset the wrong person? Had she made a mistake in her calculations?

"Your mother was a sassy witch," Eliza laughed. "And she always got her way."

"Sounds like Mom," I said. I sat down and looked at Natasha. I was ready to ask her some questions. "Eliza, can you let her speak? I have a couple of things I want to ask her."

"You mean that you don't want to wait for Helena?"

"That's what I mean."

Eliza considered the wish for a second, and then she murmured an incantation. Immediately, Natasha's mouth opened, and she acted like she was about to scream. I quickly slapped my hand over her mouth.

"Don't you dare scream," I said. "And if Helena comes in, act like you can't talk. Got it?"

Natasha nodded, and I released my hand. She looked younger now. She was wildly ageless, as most of the witches seemed to be, but right now she looked like she was in her twenties. She looked scared, and I felt a little bad.

"What do you know about Jasper?"

"Jasper? The cat?"

"He's not a cat. He's a man."

Her mouth dropped open and she shook her head.

"There's no way. He's been lurking around your Mom's house for weeks."

"For weeks?"

"Yeah," she nodded. "I thought it was your mom's cat." Then she sighed and shook her head. "I guess that's who you meant when you were talking about a shapeshifter." She looked upset that she hadn't known, and I almost felt bad for her.

Almost.

"Have you seen anyone else lurking around?"

"There's a dog that comes by sometimes," she shrugged. "But that's it."

"Did my mother ever tell you she wanted to get a pet?"

"Well, no," she shrugged.

"What about any of the other neighbors?"

"The only other person who ever talked to your mom, well, that I know of, was Fiona Wellington."

"She lives next door," Eliza supplied helpfully. "She and your mom kept a polite distance."

"Yeah, they hated each other," Natasha said.

"Why?"

Eliza sighed heavily.

"Alicia was a very kind person, and obviously, I loved her a lot, but..."

"She could be abrasive," Natasha finished for her. "She could be pretty blunt, and not everyone likes that. Oh, I didn't mind, but I'm not your normal everyday witch."

"You aren't?" I asked.

"Nope. My mom was a witch, and my dad was a polar bear shifter."

"So, can you shift into a bear?" I asked.

"No," Natasha smiled sadly. "I never learned how. My dad died when I was a kid. If I have the gene, which I'm not sure I even do, then it never seemed to unlock. Strange, right?"

"I'm sorry," I said. She seemed really disappointed.

"It's fine."

"We're trying to figure out what happened to my mom. I caught Jasper in his human form looking through her stuff."

"That son of a..." Natasha shook her head, frowning. "I am so sorry, Jaden. I didn't know. I swear it."

Somehow, I really believed her. Probably, I shouldn't have, but I did. Natasha didn't seem like a terrible person. She seemed like she actually liked her neighborhood.

And it seemed like she had really cared about my mom, albeit in a platonic sort of way. That was part of what made the next question so hard. I didn't want to hurt Eliza, but I had more questions.

"Natasha, you watch the neighborhood a lot, right?"

"Are you saying I'm a busybody?"

"No."

"Yeah, I do."

"And you see people when they're coming and going?"

"Yes."

"Did you see anyone the day my mom died?"

"Just Eliza."

"What about other days?"

"What do you mean?" She asked.

"Did you see other people come and visit my mom? Anyone regularly stop by?"

I had a theory, and I wanted to know if it was crazy. I kind of felt like I was going crazy. I wasn't sure if it was because I'd been in Which Village for a few days, or if it was because I was about to get my powers.

Natasha hesitated.

"Natasha?" Eliza pressed. "It's okay."

"I know you two were lovers," Natasha said. "I don't want to get anyone in trouble."

Eliza tensed, but nodded again.

"It's fine," she said. "Who did you see?"

"There was a man," Natasha said. "He only came about once a week."

"A man?" Eliza frowned. I knew what she was thinking. She was wondering if my mom had been unfaithful, but I didn't think that she had been. I thought it was the opposite. I understood why Eliza might be worried, though. The librarian had seen my mom with some guy she seemed to know very well, and know Natasha was basically backing that up.

"Yeah, I'm really sorry," Natasha blurted out. "I mean, I don't know what their relationship was or anything, but he only came over when it was dark out. Never in the daylight. I mean, I don't even know if I could recognize him. She hugged him though," Natasha whispered. "I probably should have said something earlier."

That confirmed my suspicions that my husband was alive, and that he'd been working with my mother. What other man would my mom hang out with? As far as I knew, she'd never had a male friend in her life. Her note, coupled with the brick through the window, made me think that my husband was lurking around Which Village and that he was giving us clues and trying to quietly help us solve my mother's murder.

What I didn't know was why.

"Jaden?" Eliza looked at me.

"I think it's what I said earlier," I whispered. I didn't want to say, "I'm pretty sure my husband faked his death." I didn't want to freak out Natasha. Besides, if Helena came barging in, I didn't want Natasha telling her all of this stuff.

But first, I needed to clarify.

Had it been Jasper that she'd seen?

Or Stanley?

"What did the man look like?" I asked gently.

"Long hair," she said.

"Are you sure it wasn't a woman?" Eliza asked.

"Definitely not. The person's build was definitely mannish."

Jasper had short hair. Stanley had short hair, too, but I hadn't seen him in months. If he'd been alive this entire time, it was possible that his hair was long now.

"What else can you tell us about the man's appearance?" I asked. I wanted to know. *Needed* to know.

"He was taller than Alicia."

"And?"

I was trying not to get impatient, but it was hard. Eliza and I were both watching as Natasha struggled to remember.

"His hair was kind of light brown, and he had normal-looking clothes. I never saw him anywhere else, so I don't think he was from around here. Oh, and he had a tattoo on his arm. Well, maybe not a tattoo. I think it was a scar of some sort."

I stilled.

"Which arm?" I asked.

Before she could answer, Eliza shot me a look that said I shouldn't push too hard. She knew exactly what I was thinking. When Stanley had died, it had been in an accident. I hadn't been able to claim his body. When the authorities contacted me regarding his death, they hadn't said much. They'd just said there had been an accident, and he was gone. Had it been a car accident? Had a tree fallen on him? Had he drowned? I didn't know. He'd gone to the shop and then on his way back he'd...

Well, he'd never made it back, and I hadn't spoken the language in that country well enough to know exactly what they were saying. He'd had scars on his left arm, though. The scars had been from a bicycle accident when he was a kid that he completely removed the skin from his limb. He'd had surgery to make things look normal again, but they hadn't.

It could have been him.

I thought I might throw up.

Just then, Helena *did* come in. Natasha wisely closed her mouth and pretended that she couldn't speak. Eliza and I looked over as Helena came into the kitchen where we were sitting. Suddenly, the room seemed a lot smaller than it had just moments ago.

"The firefighters managed to put the fire out," she said. "With a little help from me." She held up her hands proudly.

"Do you know a spell to put fires out?" I asked, curious. I still had a lot to learn about inner-workings of my mother's paranormal town.

She nodded, smiling. Helena was obviously very pleased about this, and she was more than happy to talk about herself.

"I trained for a year with a group dedicated to putting out wildfires," she explained. "We all decided that if we were going to have magical abilities, we wanted to use them for good."

"How noble."

"Thank you."

Helena looked at Natasha, then. I couldn't tell whether Helena hated Natasha or whether she was just weird and cranky. She seemed to narrow her gaze as she looked at the woman.

"Has she said anything?" She asked.

"Not yet," Eliza said. "We wanted to wait for you." Eliza's voice was calm and even. She gave away nothing. She didn't let Helena know that we'd already talked to Natasha, nor did she let on that Natasha didn't know anything. Personally, I thought the fact that they had essentially captured Natasha was really weird. This wasn't the middle ages. We could talk to people normally.

"Take the charm off," Helena ordered.

Eliza whispered something, pretending to take off the spell, and Natasha's mouth opened. She wiped it off, pretending to clear away drool, and then looked at us.

"What?" She asked. "Was that really necessary?" Natasha shook her head dramatically. "I really feel like that wasn't necessary. You could have just asked to talk to me like a normal person."

I had to admit that Natasha was a wonderful actress. She'd played her part beautifully. She'd done a great job convincing me that she was not only charmed, but that she was irritated about having Eliza put a spell on her.

"Of course, it was necessary," Helena said. "Now, explain."

"Explain what?"

"You're a busybody," Helena pointed out. Speaking of necessity, I wasn't sure if *that* was really needed. It might be true, but the words were still pretty harsh. I had basically already said the same thing to Natasha, and now, hearing those words come from Helena's mouth, I felt bad. Natasha bristled, obviously just as irritated as I was.

"Excuse me?"

"You heard me."

"Is there something that you want?" Natasha said. "Because it kind of sounds like you're only here to bully me."

"I'm here to figure out exactly what it is that you know about your neighbor's house burning down."

"I already told you that I didn't see anything."

Helena just stared. She had obviously mastered the art of waiting people out. That was important. So many people became uncomfortable with awkward silence. If you waited long enough, most of the time, someone would start talking.

They had to.

They couldn't help themselves.

At least, that had been my experience.

Natasha, however, didn't give in to Helena's obvious whims. Helena stared at Natasha, and Natasha stared right on back. Her eyes were fierce and glowing just a little bit. I wondered for a moment if there was going to be some sort of witch fight.

It seemed as though we'd come to a standstill. Helena wanted to know what Natasha had seen, and Natasha sworn she had seen nothing.

Finally, Eliza sighed.

"We aren't going to get anywhere like this," she said.

"Well, if she would just *cooperate*," Helena hissed. "Then it would be such a big deal. Would it?"

"I already told you I didn't see anything," Natasha shrugged. "I don't know what else you want from me."

"Let it go, Helena," Eliza said. She turned to Natasha. "I'm sorry for the inconvenience," she said. "We'll be leaving now."

"We'll be leaving when I say we are," Helena snapped. She glared at Eliza, and I was surprised to see how much animosity and anger she had hidden behind those eyes.

"No," Eliza said. She placed her hand on Helena's, and she stared at her sadly. "We'll be leaving now."

Something shifted in the air. I didn't know what was going on, but when we got outside, I had the feeling that I'd just seen something very important. What was I supposed to do next?

"Come on," Eliza said, glancing toward the remnants of my mother's house. "You can stay with me."

I took one last glance at the burned-down house, and then I follow Eliza to the car.

Chapter 7

I hadn't planned on staying in Eliza's huge Victorian home. It obviously doubled as her workspace, so during the day she saw clients downstairs and I hid away upstairs on the second floor. She gave me a nice little room to stay in. It was decorated with imitation flowers and beautiful paintings, and there was a big bed in the center of the room.

For an entire week, I hid away. I went over my mother's diary again and again. The notebook should have given me some sort of clue, but the truth was that I really didn't know what to do next.

I was at a loss. Eliza seemed to throw herself into her work. I didn't blame her for that, either. She had lost her girlfriend and me...

Well, I just didn't know what I was supposed to do.

I'd planned on staying in Which Village, or at least entertained the possibility of it, but maybe my mom's house burning down was some sort of cosmic sign that I shouldn't.

Could that be true?

Was there such a thing as destiny?

Perhaps most importantly, was that what I was experiencing? The world seemed a lot bigger without my mom and Stanley in it, and after a few days where *nothing* happened at all, I was starting to wonder if I'd worked myself into a frenzy for nothing.

After that first week hiding away in Eliza's house, I decided to go for a walk. She was going to be busy with clients, and I needed to get out and stretch my legs a little bit. Sitting around could be relaxing, but it could also be terrifyingly horrible.

When you were alone with your thoughts for too long, it became pretty easy to wallow in seas of regret and to start falling into endless pity parties. I didn't want to do either of those things, but I was lost.

Eliza was already meeting with someone when I reached the first floor of her house. The door to her office was closed, so I simply slipped out of the house. I was quiet, but not sneaky. I wasn't a teenager trying to sneak out of the house on a date. I was a grown woman. If I wanted to go on a walk, I could do that.

I could do anything.

Eliza's neighborhood was quiet and calm, but she lived only a few blocks from the bustling downtown of Which Village. It was still much quieter than other places I'd lived, but once I got to Main Street, there were shops and stores and a few little cafes. I passed the inn where I'd stayed that first night. I saw Lionel in the window of the lobby, and I waved. I didn't think that he saw me. If he did, he didn't wave back to me.

Strange.

Annoying.

Disappointing.

I liked to think that I was the type of person people would remember. Maybe I was, but maybe it was in all of the wrong ways. He remembered that I came to town after my mother died. I wondered how many people judged me for our failed relationship.

I stopped in a little shop and walked around, looking at all of the tiny trinkets. It was a souvenir shop of sorts.

"Can I help you, dear?" An older-looking woman stepped out from behind the counter and walked over. She was wearing a simple red dress and a long apron on the front.

"I'm okay," I said. "Just browsing."

"Getting a lot of that lately," she sighed. "Well, then, take your time."

"What do you mean?" I asked her. "What do you mean you've had a lot of that lately?" I didn't want to be too intense, but as I glanced around the shop, I couldn't help but notice I was the only one there. More than that: it looked like there hadn't been anyone else in the shop for a long time.

"It's just that there have been quite a few tourists lately," she said.

"That's strange. Here?"

"Yes, dear."

"I'm not trying to be nosy," I started.

"By all means," she waved her hand. "Nose away."

"How often do you get new visitors to your shop?" I asked. "Are there a lot of tourists who come to Which Village?"

"More than you'd think," she said. "Or maybe less." She shrugged. "We didn't have visitors for months, and then all of a sudden, they seem to be everywhere."

"I wonder why."

"Beats me."

It was a bit strange. I got the feeling that most of the residents of Which Village lived here because it was quiet and off the beaten path. People lived here because they didn't really want to have to go out of their way to hide who they were. The witches and wizards who lurked here did it because this was a place where nobody would judge them.

Nobody would hunt them down. Nobody would hurt them.

Only, somebody had.

Somebody had hurt my mother. Had it been one of the new people who'd come wandering around? Or had it been someone local? Maybe the fact that Jasper was after her werewolf potion meant something. Maybe it meant everything. I hadn't seen the cat recently. Maybe he wasn't even around anymore.

The woman in the shop was patient with me as I looked around. Finally, I grabbed a little trinket that looked unique and interesting. It was a small woodcarving of a tiny animal. It looked like a wolf, but it could have been a different kind of creature. I wasn't quite sure, but I was happy with my purchase.

"Thank you." I waved goodbye as I left the shop. The little bell on the door jingled as I left, letting the woman know that I was, in fact, leaving. Then I was outside once again, and I continued on my walk.

I went around the downtown area, taking my time looking around. Everyone seemed so *normal* in Which Village, at least at first glance. It wasn't until I was really paying attention that I started to notice the things about this place that were different.

One person walked by and kept sniffing the air. Maybe they were a wolf shifter or something like that. Perhaps they were really sensitive to different smells.

Then there was someone who kept mumbling to themselves about hexes and potions. What was it they were so worried about?

I saw a couple of people dipping into a shop that advertised as selling herbs. In a different life, I would have thought it was some sort of weed shop, but nope. It really was just a place where people could buy herbs for all of their witchy needs.

As I walked along the street, I couldn't stop thinking about how wildly my life had changed in such a short time. Less than a year ago, I'd been traveling around with Stanley. We'd been talking about settling down and not moving from place to place as much. Kids? We'd talked about it. We'd talked about getting a pet, too. There were a lot of things we'd discussed, but then he'd just...vanished.

Everyone told me he was dead. The police officers who came to explain that he was gone had said he'd been in some sort of collision. Was that a lie? Had he actually been attacked or killed by someone? Had there been an animal attack? They'd been very happy to help me leave the country quickly and without a lot of fuss.

You'll want to mourn back home.

That's what they had told me.

Now, I was toying with the idea that my husband might actually be alive and not dead. What the hell was that all about? If it was true, then part of me was horribly bothered that Stanley hadn't told me he was alive. He'd let me worry about him all on my own. He'd let me grieve and mourn and he'd let me try to move on.

The truth was that there was no moving on.

After you found true love, and after you spent your life falling for someone wonderfully special, you couldn't just "move on."

That wasn't how it worked.

Resigned that I wasn't going to find answers, I decided to head back home. Eliza would be wondering where I went, anyway. At the very least, we could eat some dinner together. I was just about to turn on the street that would lead me back to Eliza's place when I saw a flash of back in the corner of my eye.

Jasper.

I whirled around just as the cat vanished around a corner, but I didn't hesitate. I took off running, chasing him. He might be a shifter cat, but I was a witch, apparently, or about to be. I didn't know jack shit about using my powers, and I didn't really care. The only thing that mattered was getting answers.

I needed them.

We all needed them.

And so I ran.

I chased that damn cat down a street, through someone's backyard, and over a little fence. It was a good thing I ran track in high school and that Stanley had encouraged me to keep up with my running abilities. Otherwise, I might have faltered. As it was, I managed to keep up with the black cat easily.

Besides, it seemed to be slowing down.

Finally, we rounded yet another corner in the midst of suburbia, and he shifted back into his human - very naked - form. He spun around and held his hands up.

"What?" He snapped. "What could *you* possibly want from me?"

"What could I want? How about some damn answers?" I glared at him and hoped I looked scarier than I felt. What I felt like was a tiny little mouse who had gotten caught by the big bad cat. What I felt like was that I was wandering into a territory I knew nothing about. It definitely seemed like I was about to be served up to the wolves, and I didn't like that feeling very much.

Or at all.

"You?"

"What about me?"

He shook his head and laughed. It was a cold sort of laugh, and it made me feel utterly embarrassed. He thought I was stupid, I realized. Either that, or he knew something that I didn't know.

"Nothing," he said. "It's just that there's something you don't know."

There it was.

There was something I didn't know.

I was tired of being kept in the dark, too.

"Tell me."

"Or what?" He raised an eyebrow. "You'll put a spell on me?"

"Exactly right."

"You don't know any spells."

"Don't I?" I raised an eyebrow. "You've been keeping an eye on me, haven't you?"

His silence told me everything I needed to know.

"You have, huh? So, you know that I've been staying with Eliza. You know that she's a powerful witch. You know she was involved with my mother, who was also a powerful witch."

"Make your point, dolly. We don't have all day."

"I'm training under Eliza's careful watch, and I'm already twice as powerful as my mother was."

"Prove it."

"Here?" I laughed out loud and shook my head. "Nice try. I'm not about to be arrested for assaulting a cat shifter in public. Now what is it you were going to tell me?"

It was a lie.

Everything that had just come out of my mouth was a total lie.

Eliza wasn't training me.

I didn't have any powers.

I <u>definitely</u> wasn't twice the witch my mother had been.

So why had I said it?

Well, I wasn't quite sure.

I just needed to know what it was that Jasper knew. I needed to get him talking, and I needed to convince him that I was worth trusting. And fast.

"I can help you," I blurted out.

That had him interested. An eyebrow went up, and then it slowly went back down again.

"Help me, you say?"

"Nobody knows my mom better than me."

"Nobody knew, you mean."

"Cool, thanks for reminding me that she's dead."

I turned and walked away. It was a bluff. I was irritated that he'd brought it up, but not enough that I was going to give up a chance at answers.

Sure enough, my bullshit paid off. I felt a hand on my shoulder, and I turned out.

"Not here," he said.

"Then where?"

"Tonight at midnight," he said. "Meet me at your mom's place."

"But it's burned down," I started to say, but he had already changed into his cat form. He meowed loudly, and then he ran away, bounding down the street. Just then, a car drove by, and I turned and kept walking, trying to ignore the growing dread in my stomach.

I was supposed to meet a cat shifter at midnight at the place where my mom had died.

What could possibly go wrong?

"SOMETHING'S DIFFERENT about you this evening," Eliza said, looking at me. We were eating dinner together. It was a simple meal of grilled cheese sandwiches and raw carrots, but I didn't mind. I hadn't felt like cooking, and apparently, Eliza *never* cooked.

"I've been thinking about my mother."

It was a half-truth. The whole truth was that I'd been thinking about who killed my mother and I was ready to go find them. That truth meant I was going to have to face whoever thought it was okay to kill a poor little witch who wasn't causing problems for anyone.

Well, I guessed that wasn't quite true.

She had been causing problems, hadn't she?

My mother had been causing a lot of problems for people. She'd been causing a lot of chaos in town with her hexes and her potions and her desire to find a solution to werewolves and their ability to shift.

"What about her?" Eliza asked carefully.

"When do you think my powers will come in?"

"What do you mean?"

"Well, you said witches in my family get their powers on their birthday, right?"

"Their 35th birthday."

"Yes."

I gestured around the room and then at myself.

"You aren't 35 yet."

"I've been 35 for two hours and nothing's happened," I pointed out.

"It's your birthday?"

"As of 4:00 this afternoon, yes."

"You didn't tell me that."

I looked at her.

"Was I supposed to have told you that?"

Eliza sighed and shook her head.

"It kind of seems like you're keeping secrets from me, little witch."

"Not at all," I said. "It's just that I'm not really sure what you want from me. More than that: I'm not sure what you *need* from me."

"Honesty."

"Okay, I'm honestly 35. When should I expect my powers to appear?" I asked. "Am I supposed to do something? Is there like, a ceremony I'm supposed to partake in?"

Eliza looked at me carefully. She set down the last bite of her grilled cheese sandwich. Her baby carrots were left untouched. She cocked her head carefully, looking at me like she was searching for answers herself.

"I don't know."

Okay, not the answer I was looking for.

"What do you mean?"

"I mean, I don't know," she shrugged. "I was born a witch, love. I've always had powers. Women like your mom are rare."

"That doesn't seem very fair."

"I suppose it's not."

"Did she ever tell you how she knew she was a witch?"

"We didn't talk about it a lot," Eliza admitted. "Your mother was a very private person."

"Mom? Private? I'm shocked," I said lamely. Private didn't even begin to describe the way my mother acted. She was so far past private that it was crazy.

My mother wasn't exactly self-absorbed, but she was pretty damn close. I didn't judge her for running off the way that she did. I was just frustrated that even in death, I was missing her. She was dead, and I still couldn't get answers. This time, I couldn't get answers that I seriously *needed*.

I needed to know what was going to happen to me. I needed to know how I could get my powers. It wasn't hard for me to believe that I was a witch in my heart. I'd seen so many wonderful, strange, and incredible things on my journeys throughout the world.

To me, this just seemed like another journey.

It was something new, and something undiscovered, and it was something that I desperately needed.

"I'm sorry I'm not more helpful," Eliza finally said. "We can go to the library tomorrow, if you like. Maybe we can find some more books."

"Maybe," I said noncommittally.

"Have you had a chance to look through your mother's notebook?" She asked, reaching for a carrot.

"What about it?"

"I was wondering if there were any notes in it about your upcoming transformation from human girl to witch goddess."

"The only stuff I've read in there is the stuff about the potion she was working on. Honestly, there wasn't anything helpful."

"Pity," she said.

"I agree."

We finished eating in silence, and then Eliza and I loaded the dishwasher and went our separate ways. She went to her office to finish some work for the evening, and I went upstairs to relax and read before I went to meet up with Jasper. Mostly, I wanted to avoid the weird talking plants in her office.

Besides, I wasn't going to tell Eliza about my outing. After all, it wasn't really any of her business. I was an adult woman, and I could leave the house if I wanted to. It felt strange, living with someone else. It was past time for me to make a decision about my future. I'd had a week to think about it, but I still had a lot of questions about what happened to my mother.

I promised myself that once I'd solved the mystery of what happened to Mom, I'd decide whether Which Village was the kind of place I could grow old in. Maybe it was a place I really would want to stay forever, but maybe not.

But I needed my own place.

I made a mental note to start looking for houses or short-term rentals the next day. As soon as I did that, I could get my own space, and I could spread out, and I could relax, and I could make some plans for how I wanted to start living my life.

Mom was dead.

She wasn't coming back.

It was time for me to start dealing with it.

As soon as it was time for me to meet Jasper, I grabbed my phone and shoved it into my back pocket. I had my wallet in the other pocket. My car keys went into my front pocket, and I looked at the bedroom window.

Should I sneak out?

For just a moment, I considered it. The truth was, though, that this wasn't a 90s rom-com. I wasn't a teenager trying to sneak out on a date. I was a grownup. More than that, I was a widow. Possibly. If I wanted to go for a drive, I could. Eliza couldn't stop me, and somehow, I also thought that she wouldn't.

Her bedroom door was closed, and when I got downstairs, I saw that her office door was, too. The lights were off. She'd gone to bed, I suspected, and I headed outside to my car.

Eliza didn't have any sort of alarm system on her house, which was weird to me. She'd given me a key to the front door, though, and I locked it before getting in the car and driving off.

For just a moment, I wondered if I needed to be concerned about being followed by anyone lurking around in the darkness, but I quickly brushed that off.

It was a stupid idea, really.

Nobody was going to follow someone like me around town. Nobody. I didn't know nearly enough about life in this world, and I certainly didn't know enough about my mother to inspire someone to follow me. The idea was sort of silly, actually.

I made it to my mom's place in record time, but I still parked down the street. I wasn't sure if Natasha was home tonight, but I didn't want to risk alerting her and her nosy eyes as to someone hanging out at Mom's.

Quietly, I got out of the car and closed the door. I locked the car, but cringed as it beeped and the lights flickered, reaving my existence to anyone who might be paying even the slightest bit of attention.

"Shit," I muttered. I paused, waiting for someone to notice me, but nobody did. As soon as I was certain that I was safe, I started walking toward the house.

When I reached it, I looked over the damage, assessing the situation. Despite the fact that it was midnight, I could see the house. The moon was bright. Which Village always seemed to have a really bright moon.

"It's charmed," a voice said from behind me. I turned around to see Jasper standing there. Unlike our previous encounters, he was fully dressed this time.

"Excuse me?" I said.

"The moon. I noticed you staring at it," he explained. "It's charmed."

"What does that mean?"

"It means someone wanted it to look bigger, so they made it look bigger."

"I guess that makes sense."

"So, you're Alicia's daughter."

"That's what they tell me."

"What else do they tell you?" He asked carefully.

"What do you mean?"

I wasn't really in the mood for games, but I knew perfectly well that I was going to have to play some in order to get the information I needed. The truth was that Jasper knew *something* about my mom's disappearance. He might not know what it was that he knew, but he knew it all the same.

Now I needed his help.

More than anything else, I needed to know what had happened to her, why she'd been killed. I needed to know what was so important about her research that someone would want to silence her.

And then there was Stanley.

I didn't want to tell anyone out loud that I thought my late husband was back from the dead. This might be a wizarding sort of place, but I knew enough to know that seeing dead people? That was a fast way to end up in a hospital. Eliza hadn't had me committed, but maybe she had been simply being nice. Perhaps she'd been doing me a favor because of her relationship with my mom.

"You've been spending a lot of time with Eliza."

"Yeah."

"What has she told you about your mother?"

I looked over at the ashen remains of my mom's house. Jasper turned, looking at it, too. We were standing to the side of where it used to be, and we were partially obstructed from view by a couple of bushes.

"Walk with me," he said.

"Where?"

"Let's walk away from here. Never know who might be watching."

He jerked his head toward Natasha's house, and I shrugged. We started walking down the driveway and then to the sidewalk. Then we made our way down the street, away from familiar houses and watchful eyes.

"Why did you ask me about Eliza?" I wanted to know. I shoved my hands in my jean pockets. Now that Jasper and I were alone, and now that he was actually dressed for the first time ever, things felt a little more comfortable.

He didn't seem quite so scary.

"There's a lot about Which Village you don't know," he said.

"Then why don't you fill me in? No offense, but my mom is dead, you're super sus, and you have no idea what I'm capable of."

"Ah," he said. "Is that a threat, little witch?"

"I'm not little."

"Nor are you a witch."

"Excuse me?"

"You don't have your powers yet."

Silence fell. I stopped walking and turned and looked at Jasper. He knew. Somehow, and I didn't know how, he knew that I was a total fraud. I really *didn't* have my powers yet, but how could he possibly know that?

"Who the hell are you?" I whispered.

He smiled, grinning brightly, and stuck his hand out.

"Jasper Jacobson," he said. "It's a pleasure to meet you."

Chapter 8

J asper shook his head when he realized I wasn't about to shake his hand.

"Pity," he said. "We could have been so great, you and I."

"Stop stalling," I said. I put my hands on my hips and looked at him. We were in the middle of some random neighborhood by that point, and I was certain that if anyone looked outside and saw us, they'd think it was some sort of domestic dispute and they'd come kill us.

"You want me to give it to you straight?"

"Please."

"Your powers will come naturally on your birthday."

"Okay."

That was in two days. I wasn't really sure why I'd lied to Eliza about my powers or about my birthday. I was starting to feel a little uncomfortable around her, but I hadn't been able to pinpoint why. There was just too much information to deal with, yet at the same time, not nearly enough.

"You haven't told anyone you don't have your abilities yet," Jasper said.

"No."

"Why not?"

I was silent.

"You don't trust Eliza," he said.

"That's ridiculous. She was my mother's lover."

"Was she?" He asked.

"Excuse me?"

"Was she your mother's lover?"

"What do you mean?" I asked, staring at him.

"Did your mother ever mention Eliza when she spoke with you?"

No.

She never had.

She had been wildly private. Besides, my mother and I had barely spoken at all. She had been invested in her own life and I'd been invested in mine. Things had been simpler that way.

But was he trying to say that Eliza had lied about her relationship?

I decided that I needed to take charge of the conversation and the direction that it was going. Jasper was trying his best to confuse me and get me wound up. That wasn't going to be very good for me.

"Who are you working for?" I asked. "Why don't we start with that?"

"I'm a shapeshifter."

"Yeah, I got that."

"I live with other shapeshifters."

"Okay?"

"And one thing that shapeshifters really hate is having to deal with werewolves."

"Okay."

"We don't like the fact that they give all shifters a bad name."

"Explain to me the difference again. Please."

"Shapeshifters are born this way," Jasper explained.

"Can you shift into anything?"

"No. Each person can change into their destined animal shape, and then back into their human form. That's it."

So, he could be a cat, or he could be a man. Got it.

"And werewolves are different from you how? What's the difference between a wolf shapeshifter and a werewolf?" That was the part that was so tricky and wild to me.

"See that full moon?"

I looked up at the moon. It was so bright, and so beautiful, and so wonderful.

"Have you ever wondered why there is a full moon almost every single night in Which Village?"

I had. It didn't seem scientifically possible. Then again, a lot of things didn't seem scientifically possible, but that hadn't stopped anyone from going nuts in town.

"Yes."

"It's charmed."

"I believe you mentioned that."

He rolled his eyes.

"Look, it's charmed because people want to force werewolves out of hiding. Werewolves can't control when they shift. If there's a full moon, and the moonlight touches a werewolf at all, he'll change into his monster form. He can't control himself in that form."

"But shifters can."

"You know that we can."

"Why would anyone want to force werewolves out of hiding?"

"Because people in Which Village don't like werewolves," he said. "The people here believe in a type of magic that only applies to the select chosen ones."

"Meaning?"

"Meaning if you aren't a witch or a wizard around here, you're considered trash."

"But you're a shapeshifter. Do they think you're crazy?"

"Do you *see* any friends around me?" He gestured. "The only reason I'm not dead is because people thought I was your mom's pet."

"Do you know what happened to her?"

"No," he said. "But I do know that Eliza isn't telling you everything."

"How do you know that?"

"Because she's the one who paid me to go through your mom's stuff," he said. He looked around wildly, then, and cocked his head as though he had heard something. "Time for me to go."

He shifted into his cat form, then, and his clothes were just a pile on the ground. I stared at them for a second before realizing that there was no way I was going to leave clothing on the middle of the sidewalk. I picked it up and dropped it behind a bush. If Jasper wanted to come back for it later, he could.

Then I kept walking.

I'd only made it a few more feet when, sure enough, someone came around the corner. The bright lights of a car were on me and slowed down as they approached. I raised my arm, covering my eyes, and when the car stopped, I lowered my hand.

"Eliza?" I asked when I saw her.

"I was so worried," she said. "Is everything okay?"

"Yeah," I said. "I just went out to clear my head."

"All the way across town?" She raised an eyebrow.

"Yeah," I said. "I couldn't sleep, and I do my best thinking at night."

"I see," she said. It looked like she didn't believe me. "Well, if you're sure you're okay."

"I'm fine," I said. "I'll be back when I'm done."

"Just lock up when you come inside."

"You got it."

She drove away slowly, and I watched as her car disappeared around the corner.

Was Jasper right?

Was there more to Eliza than met the eye?

I didn't like the idea that he could be right about my mother's passing. I also didn't like the idea that I had somehow been tricked by Eliza. The problem was that I didn't have anyone I could turn to or ask.

Stanley was gone and my mother...well, she was really gone.

I went back to my car, and I drove back to Eliza's house. When I parked, I thought I saw movement at one of the windows. Was she waiting up for me? Watching?

I went into the house, up to my bedroom, and climbed into bed without taking off my clothes. The next day, I'd find somewhere else to live. It was time.

AS IT TURNED OUT, THERE weren't many short-term rentals in Which Village, so I found myself back at the inn. While Eliza was a little upset at losing her roommate, I explained that I needed some space until the funeral. Once that happened, things would be a little calmer, I assured her. I also promised that we'd meet up for regular lunch dates.

Eliza wanted to know if I was going to continue to look for my mother's killer.

"No," I lied. "I think that we'll let the police work on that."

She seemed like she didn't believe me, but that was fine. Eliza didn't seem like the kind of person who was going to push, and I was happy with that.

The truth was that the inn was fine. I still didn't understand all of the magic surrounding it. How was it possible that the insides of the cabins seemed so much bigger than the outside? How was it that everything always smelled perfect?

Perhaps most importantly, how was it that everything inside the little rental was so wildly calming?

On the eve of my birthday, I sat in the cabin with a little cupcake I'd purchased at a corner shop, and I lit a tiny candle. I didn't sing to myself or anything ridiculous like that, but I did make a birthday wish.

"I wish Stanley was here," I whispered out loud.

I looked around the room, as though that would change anything. There was nothing, though. There was no *whoosh* of excitement. There was no wind. The lights didn't flicker. Everything was just entirely the time.

I went ahead and blew out the candle, ate my cupcake, and crawled into bed. I laid there for what seemed like an eternity. I still had so many questions. What had happened to my mom? How was I going to find out who killed her? When was I going to get my powers?

After a long time, I finally got out of bed and sat down with her notebook. I went over it again. I'd read the words a million times. She had potions in there and notes about the shapeshifter stuff, but as I read it this time, I noticed something else.

There were extra words.

In between each line, there was a thin, silver string of words that hadn't been there before.

Either that, or I hadn't been *able* to see it before.

"Mom?" I whispered. "What the hell did you do?"

As I read the notebook that time, I wondered if I was able to see the extra words because I was officially 35. I was officially a witch. Did that mean that my powers had come in? Could I *do* things now? Why hadn't Eliza seen the other words? Maybe she had, and she just hadn't told me, or perhaps this was something special I could only see because I was my mother's daughter.

I read the notebook again, and this time, it seemed very different. There were still the recipes and the information about her ideas regarding shapeshifters, but there were other things, too.

There were notes about the people in town. She talked about who supported werewolves and who was against them.

And there was a lot of information about Mr. Quartz.

Stanley.

So, he was alive.

As soon as I read the entry about his arrival in Which Village, I ran to the bathroom and puked. I threw up for about ten minutes, and then I sat beside the toilet and thought about what I'd learned. Okay, so I'd suspected for awhile that he was still alive, but now I knew that he *actually* was. He was alive, and he was...

Somewhere.

Well, he'd been in Which Village before my mom died. Her notebook said all sorts of stuff about that. If I was reading things correctly, he'd come to her for help.

I just didn't know why.

I crawled out of the bathroom and back to the notebook. I didn't trust walking. That wasn't going to work for me. My new powers, so far, were not exactly wild and wicked the way I'd imagined them to be, but I could read secret invisible writing. That had to count for something.

I picked up the notebook and started reading.

"So that was what happened," I whispered.

He'd been bitten.

It hadn't been a collision. The police had lied. It was an animal attack after all. What was worse? The animal attack that had "killed" him hadn't killed him at all. He'd been bitten by a werewolf while we were away, and he'd run off and gotten lost.

He hadn't returned to our lodging. He hadn't been able to find me. I'd moved back to America almost immediately after his disappearance, and he hadn't been able to find me. He'd had a hard time learning to get his werewolf mood swings under control. Every time there was a full moon, he'd change, and he'd wake up somewhere new.

Apparently, when he was in his werewolf form, he couldn't remember anything.

He had looked for me.

I felt sick when I realized that he'd searched. He'd tried. He'd been lost and alone and scared, and he'd tried to find me. The authorities had been so happy to send me back to America and get me off of their foreign soil. I'd thought that there was nothing left for me there.

I'd been wrong.

And he'd been lost.

"Stanley, where are you?" I whispered. He'd managed to find my mom. Judging from her notes, she was trying to find a way for him to control his shifting. Once she helped him, she was going to come find me. She was going to get us back together.

"Well, shit."

I leaned back against the wall and shook my head. I'd missed him. I'd missed both of them. I hadn't gotten to my mom in time to save her, and I hadn't known that Stanley was still alive.

Somehow, I knew that it was going to be a long-ass night.

I forced myself to finish going through the journal. I was hoping there would be more great reveals, but it was all very monotonous stuff. There was the occasional note about how she'd realized she was a witch, and there were a few tiny spells written in the margins of the book.

Maybe I'd try one.

After all, what could it hurt?

One of the spells was supposed to be something you could do to reveal things you'd lost. Another was for making your hair look incredible. My mom had even included a spell for retrieving a pen.

I'd start with that one.

I was holding the notebook and sitting on the bed. Next to the bed was a small nightstand, and there was a pen on top of it. I looked at the book in front of me, and then I stared at the pen. I held up my hand, pointed at the pen, and whispered *dongbi*.

I focused on bringing my entire body to life. I needed this more than anything else. I *needed* this win. I needed to have something that I could claim as my own. I needed to feel like my life hadn't been a waste and that I hadn't lost everything for nothing.

"Please," I whispered.

I held my hand out again.

For a moment, I thought the pen moved. It didn't, though, and I felt like I was screwing this up beyond belief.

"It's just a simple spell," I said out loud. "How can it not work?"

I took a deep breath, tried to clear my mind, and tried again.

And again.

And again.

Nothing worked.

I tried standing, sitting, and lying down. I tried spinning in a circle before I whispered the words, and I tried drinking some water and then trying again, but nothing.

There was nothing.

"What am I missing?" I asked aloud. I stared at the pen, and I stared at the notebook in my hand, and finally, I dropped the notebook on the bed and looked at the pen.

For me, this was the ultimate test of whether I'd actually grown as a person. Had I learned anything? Had I figured out what it was going to take to solve the mystery of mom's death?

"I don't know who did this, Mom," I said, staring at the pen. "But I'm going to figure it out."

Then I thrust my hands forward, and I screamed at the pen. *DONGBI.*

It flew off the nightstand and into my hands.

I had done it.

It was time to solve a murder.

Chapter 9

When I left the inn for breakfast the next day, I stopped by the office to talk with Leslie and Lionel.

"Thanks for giving me a place to stay," I said.

"You're paying for it," Lionel grunted. "It's hardly us doing you any favors."

Still, he seemed to smile a little to himself, and that made me feel better. So he *did* like me.

"Can I ask you both something?"

"Sure," Leslie shrugged. She pushed her glasses up the end of her nose. "What is it?"

"Someone said something to me when I was downtown," I explained. "They told me there have been a lot of newcomers to Which Village. Do you know what that's about?"

Leslie and Lionel exchanged glances. Was it just me, or did they look worried?

"No," Leslie said, shaking her head. "I'm afraid that we don't."

She shrugged, as though she regretted not being able to help me more, and I fought the feeling of disappointment that threatened to overwhelm me.

"Okay," I said. I knew she was lying, but I wasn't going to push it. Only, Lionel was watching me intently, and he walked around me, went to the lobby door, and locked it. Then he turned back around.

"Lionel?" Leslie said. "What is it?"

"She's Alicia's daughter," he said. "Maybe she can help. If anyone can, it's her."

"That might be true," Leslie said carefully.

"You do know something," I said.

Lionel reached behind the registration desk and pulled out a little card. It was no bigger than a business card, and it had a picture of a werewolf beneath a full moon. On the back of the card was an advertisement.

IT'S WEREWOLF SEASON IN WHICH VILLAGE. COME CATCH ONE OF YOUR OWN TO SHOW THE FAM. BIGGEST BAG OF THE SEASON WINS A PRIZE.

I thought I was going to be sick.

"People are hunting them?"

"Yes," he said.

"Does this happen often?"

"I've lived in Which Village for nearly a hundred years, Jaden. I've never seen anything like this before."

He shook his head sadly, and I stared at the card some more.

"Someone is trying to draw newcomers to town," I said.

"And they're doing a good job of it," Leslie said. "The cabins are rented for the next month."

"Are you serious?"

They both nodded, blinking.

"Has that ever happened before?"

"Never," Leslie said. Now that they were bringing me in on this information, she seemed eager to share. "We've been running this inn for years. We're never booked that far out."

"So do you think someone is trying to rid the town of werewolves or bring in tourists?" I asked.

"Could be both," Lionel said.

"Could be neither," Leslie said.

Lionel turned, glaring at her.

"Neither? Not neither. It's definitely one or the other, Leslie. You saw the card just as well as I did. Someone wants people here. It's just a matter of figuring out who."

"Well, maybe it's a distraction of some sort," she said.

"A distraction?" I asked.

"Yes," she nodded. "You know, your mother was a wonderful person, but she also rankled people sometimes."

"I can't imagine that," I said dryly.

"I know it's hard to believe," Leslie kept talking, not getting the sarcasm in my voice. "But sometimes, people were upset when she shared her ideas."

"What sort of ideas?"

"She'd almost finished her cure for werewolves," Lionel told me. "She only needed someone to test it on, but she said she'd found someone."

Stanley.

She'd found Stanley.

Only, she hadn't gotten the chance to test it on him because something else had happened first, hadn't it? Someone had killed her before she'd been able to use it, and now the potion was unfinished and untested.

Who *wouldn't* want werewolves cured?

Who would want them hunted instead?

I realized who it was almost immediately, and my stomach tossed and turned.

"Lionel, Leslie," I said, lowering my voice. "How many people know about the business card? Did you tell anyone else?"

"Only the mayor," Leslie said. "I called her just a few minutes before you got here. You know, in case she wanted to raise awareness about safety. If we're going to have an influx of visitors, then people need to know how to protect themselves."

"You told the mayor," I whispered.

"Is something wrong?" Leslie asked.

"I'm pretty sure she's the one who killed my mom."

Saying it out loud felt forced and strange. The words seemed to catch in my throat.

"She wanted tourists to come to town, and she hated werewolves."

"Helena Porridge is an old bat," Lionel said. It was funny coming from him. He looked much older than her. "And she's always been cranky."

"Why doesn't she like werewolves?"

"Her brother was bitten by one," Leslie said. "Years ago. She doesn't talk about it."

"What happened to the brother?"

"Nobody knows," she said. "But ever since then, she's been careful not to talk about them. It's only the older people who probably remember that, anyway."

"Did my mother know that Helena hated werewolves?"

They shook their heads.

"Most people didn't know," Lionel said. "Whether you like or hate werewolves isn't something people say too much. The only opinion people have is whether to show up to the monthly charming session where the moon is re-charmed."

"That takes a group?"

"Absolutely. No one witch is that strong. Well, Eliza could probably do it," he chuckled. "But she's a strong witch, isn't she?"

Was she?

I had no way to know, but if that was true, then we were going to need her. There was no doubt that Helena was on her way to the inn, and she was going to try to silence Lionel and Leslie. She'd obviously worked hard to keep the town's new tourist revival a secret. She wasn't going to let them just run their mouths.

"Can I use your phone?" I asked.

I dialed Eliza's number, happy that I'd memorized it, and she answered on the first ring.

"Leslie?"

"It's Jaden," I corrected her.

"Oh."

"Listen, I need to ask you something."

"Okay."

"Did you pay Jasper to find my mom's werewolf potion recipe?"

Silence, and then she breathed a big sigh of...something.

"Yes," she said. "I wanted to make sure her research wasn't lost forever."

"Why didn't you tell me sooner?"

"To be honest, Jaden, I didn't know if I could trust you."

"You came to the house," I said. "You acted like you didn't know him."

"I couldn't give away all of my secrets at once, now could I?"

"You should have told me."

"What's this really about?"

"Helena," I said.

"I knew it!"

"Lionel and Leslie found a card advertising a werewolf hunting event," I said. Then, nothing. There was nothing. "Hello?" I asked, but the line was dead.

I looked over at Lionel and Leslie and nodded.

"She's here," I said.

"Or about to be," Leslie whispered.

I didn't know what the rules were for a magical fight. Was this the sort of thing that went "to the death"? I had no clue. All I knew was that whatever was about to happen was going to change everything I knew about magic.

Forever.

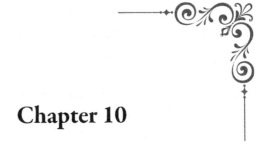

Chapter 10

When I was a little girl, my mother always told me to pay attention to the things I couldn't see.

Sometimes, the most important things are the ones you don't look at.

That was part of the problem I'd had. I'd been caught off-guard by the wonders and mystery surrounding the village that I hadn't paid attention to the most important thing: people lie.

Eliza hadn't killed my mother, but she'd kept important information from me: information that may have been able to help me figure things out earlier than I actually had. Then again, maybe I needed to go through the process of confronting Jasper, of discovering the secret room beneath the library, and finding my mom's journal.

Life truly was a journey, and sometimes the only way through the fire was *straight* through.

I walked outside of the inn. Part of me expected something wild and crazy: like a darkened sun or a thunderstorm or lightning bolts that were shooting out of the sky.

None of that happened.

Instead, I saw Helena walking toward the front of the inn. She'd parked over by the cabins. Had she had time to cut the telephone lines? Maybe it was just a misunderstanding.

"Of course, you're here," she shook her head. "Why is it that you always seem to be in the midst of trouble?"

"I could ask you the same question."

"This is my town," she said, cocking her head. "It's my job to be aware of the comings and goings of the residents."

"And to bring in tourists?" I asked, raising an eyebrow.

"Tourism is part of what keeps our village alive," she said. "Although it's been dying lately."

"That's not the only thing that's been dying," I said. "You killed my mother."

I said it out loud and let the words hang in the air between us. It was just Helena and me outside in the parking lot of the inn. Lionel and Leslie were both still inside, but I knew they were watching through the windows.

"That's quite an accusation," Helena said. She seemed nonplussed, as though it was no concern of hers.

"How did you do it?" I whispered. "Did you put a spell on her?"

Eliza had said it was a hex. I didn't know if that was true. If it was, it was horrifying to me. If not, well, there were other ways to die that were just as horrible. I knew that there was no such thing as a magic spell that could just kill someone. You had to actually *do* something. Unless you were deep into dark magic, you could curse an object that would cause harm or trick someone into eating something poisoned, but just casting a killing spell?

That couldn't be done.

Not as far as I knew.

"Do you know how I became the coven leader of this town?" Helena asked, crossing her arms over her chest.

"That's not what we're talking about."

"I think it's time for you to shut up," she pinched her fingers closed, and my mouth snapped shut, "and listen." She smiled at me, and I realized she'd cast the silencing spell on me. It was the same one that Eliza had used on Natasha.

I tried to talk, to scream, but nothing happened. I whirled around, only to see that Lionel and Leslie were banging on the windows of the inn. They were trapped inside and couldn't get out.

"They're a bit busy," Helena said, smiling menacingly at me. "They won't be coming out."

She circled around me like a vulture, like I was prey. We were still in the parking lot, and I wondered what it meant that she wasn't taking me somewhere more private. Maybe she wasn't going to kill me. Only, I knew I wasn't going to be so lucky. I knew that whatever was going to happen next was going to change everything, and it wasn't going to be what I wanted.

The truth was that I wanted my powers. Okay, so I could move a pen. That was something. Next, I needed to be able to do more things: bigger things. Those were skills I'd have to learn over time. Right now, I couldn't do that.

I couldn't do anything.

The coven leader of Which Village was here, and she was ready to take me down. There was no doubt in my mind that she had a way of hexing me just like she hexed my mother.

"Your mom had a soft heart," Helena said. "That was always her problem. She was weak."

Maybe that was true.

"She wanted to save everyone, including the werewolves." Helena made a gagging sound, as though this was the grossest thing she'd ever heard. "Can you believe it? Werewolves."

I shook my head, trying to break the curse that kept my mouth shut. Where was a wild shapeshifting cat when I needed one? If Jasper was around, he'd be able to distract Helena so I could get away.

As it was, I was all alone.

It was just me versus Helena, and I had a feeling I was going to lose this battle.

"Your mom was kind of a busybody," Helena continued her rant. "She was secretive and weird and no matter how many times I told her not to create a potion to *save the werewolves*, she couldn't help herself. It was horrible, really. Who does that? Nobody needs to *save* a werewolf. We only need to be free of them."

I watched, waiting. Eliza hadn't shown up, and neither had Japser, and the innkeepers were still stuck inside.

So this was it.

This was how I was going to die.

I'd come so close to solving the mystery of my mother's death, but in the end, I'd completely botched it, hadn't I? I'd made the mistake of thinking I could be brave, or that my powers would magically present themself.

It hadn't happened.

I tried again to scream.

Nothing.

I thought of my mom and how much I missed her.

Nothing.

Then I thought of Stanley.

I thought of the way he looked on our wedding day, and I thought of the way he always smiled at me and told me that he believed in me. I thought of all of the memories I'd missed out on with him, and I thought of how much I missed him.

And I screamed.

And my voice was loud.

Helena looked shocked as I managed to break the seal of her magic and to scream loudly at her.

"H-H-How?" She whispered. She looked at her hands and back at me, as though they were somehow going to give her the answer that she was looking for.

"You killed my mother," I whispered. "It was you this whole time."

I opened my mouth to scream again, but before I could, she started shaking her head.

"Stop!" She yelled. "Don't do that again!"

"Nothing she could have done could have been bad enough to murder over," I shouted. "Nothing!"

"You don't know what it's like!"

"And now I never will."

I saw something move from behind one of the cabins. Helena's back was to them, and she couldn't see them, but I could, and I wasn't scared. It was the monster I thought existed, but I hadn't been able to find.

The werewolf who crept toward Helena was big, towering over both of us. It must have been close to eight feet tall, if not taller. It was easy to see why the magic users in town didn't like the werewolves coming around.

I understood why she wanted to hunt them.

But I also understood that she was wrong.

My mother had been right. Someone who couldn't control their ability to shift should be helped – not condemned. Helena had every chance to change her mind about killing innocent weres, but she hadn't.

She'd fought to the bitter end, and now it was her time.

She noticed me staring behind her, and she turned just as the werewolf reached her.

"No," she shook her head. She raised her hands and started to whisper a spell, but it was too late, and he was too close. It was so early in the morning that the charmed moon of Which Village was still bright in the sky, and the wolf was still wildly strong and wickedly fast.

The werewolf raised his paw, and he brought his claws down across Helena's throat. She fell to the ground without a fight, and she laid there, completely still.

I didn't have to look at her to know that she was totally, completely dead. I also didn't regret the fact that she had died. She'd killed my mom, after all. She'd committed murder. If the werewolf hadn't shown up when he had, she was going to kill me, too, and then probably Leslie and Lionel. He'd saved us all.

I looked up to thank him, and when I saw his eyes, I stopped moving.

I knew those eyes.

"Stanley?" I whispered, biting my lip. It had to be him. I had to believe it was him.

The werewolf just stared at me.

"You're the one who threw the rock, aren't you?" I asked.

He nodded.

"You wanted me to find you."

Again, a nod.

"I missed you," I said.

The werewolf looked like he wanted terribly to talk to me, but he couldn't. This seemed to infuriate him, and with a growl, he turned and ran off into the surrounding forests, and I was left alone.

Eliza pulled into the parking lot just as the werewolf disappeared between the trees. At the same time, Lionel and Leslie seemed to be able to leave the inn, and they came over immediately.

Everyone started talking at once. Nobody could believe what had happened. A werewolf, in town. Can you believe it? Nobody could believe it.

I could, though.

I knew that werewolf, and he had saved me more than once, and he probably would again soon.

"Are you okay?" Eliza asked, and I nodded even though I didn't think it was true.

He was alive, and he was in Which Village, but how was I going to find him? Stanley had been my everything for as long as I could remember. Now that we'd found and caught my mother's killer, I wanted to find *him*.

"You're safe now," Eliza said, wrapping her arms around me. "We all are."

"The police are on their way," Leslie said. She held up a cell phone, showing us that she'd been able to reach someone.

"We'll need to get a new mayor," Lionel grumbled.

"Eliza would make a good one," Leslie pointed out.

"Me?" Eliza looked up sharply. "I don't know if I'd make a good mayor," she said. "I'm just glad that Helena received the justice she deserved."

I hugged Eliza, pulling her close, and I whispered the same thing to her that she'd said to me minutes earlier.

"You're safe now," I told her. "And everything's going to be okay."

Epilogue

I stood in front of the space where the house was being constructed. It was lovely, and I couldn't quite believe it was going to be mine. Eliza and Natasha stood on either side of me, looking at the house. It wasn't anywhere close to being finished, but we could all imagine exactly what it was going to look like when it was done.

Eliza had the floor plans for my mom's home, so I was literally having the same house built in the same spot. It might be weird or morbid, but it was sort of my way of celebrating my mom. It also gave me a great excuse to be close to the village while I tried to figure out where my husband had run off to.

If my mother's notes were true, then Stanley didn't remember things that happened in his werewolf form. When he was a human, he only knew things that he'd experienced as a human. That meant he might not remember that he'd found me. He might not even remember that he'd saved me or that he'd sought vengeance on my mother's killer.

"It's going to be beautiful," Eliza said.

"You'll make a great neighbor," Natasha added.

"Thanks," I said. "I hope it's everything I've ever dreamed it could be."

"She'd be proud of you, you know," Eliza said.

"I like to think that," I agreed. I didn't know if I'd done anything worth being proud of, but I tried my best to stay strong and make good choices, and I knew that with my new friends, we'd be able to change the world together, starting with Which Village.

"Hey, it's the mayor," an old woman yelled from next door.

"Hi Fiona," Eliza waved. She'd been a shoe-in for the position. Fiona was going to be my next-door neighbor, and even though she hadn't liked my mother very much, she seemed to like me okay. That was good news for me. It meant that my life was going to be a lot easier than I thought.

"I'd like to talk with you about noise ordinances," Fiona said, walking over. She jerked her head toward the property in front of us. "Because the construction here is quite loud, and it disturbs me."

"Well, I'd be happy to discuss this with you," Eliza said.

"You would?"

"Absolutely. Why don't we have tea together tomorrow at my office?"

Fiona nodded happily and went back to her house. Natasha and I just stared at Eliza.

"You're going to have tea?"

"To talk about the noise?" Natasha added. "Those construction workers are the quietest ones I've ever been around. Trust me when I say that the loudest thing on our block is her."

"It's all politics," Eliza waved her hand. "Besides, it gives me something to do and someone to eat with now that my roommate is gone."

"Sorry about that," I blushed. I was still staying at the inn. I liked having my space, and the truth was that Eliza did, too. I still came over once a week for lunch and to talk about ways I could find my husband. I'd started really searching for him, and I'd even bought some books on werewolf hunting. Not that I planned on hunting him, but if I was going to find a werewolf, I needed to know where to start.

I closed my eyes for a moment and took a deep breath. One adventure had ended. I'd figured out who hurt my mom, and I'd learned that I am actually a witch. Now it was time to start solving the next mystery of my life.

Where was my husband?

And why couldn't I find him?

"Hang on, Stanley," I whispered. "I'll find you."

It was a promise.

THE END

For updates on future releases and to read the next story when it is released, please follow L.C. Mortimer on her Facebook page: www.facebook.com/authorlcmortimer

Author

L.C. Mortimer loves books almost as much as she loves coffee. When she's not on a caffeine-induced writing spree, she can be found pole dancing, traveling, or playing with her pet hamster, Neko. Mortimer loves reading, playing video games, and spending time with her husband and kids. Please make sure to join her mailing list here.[1]

---

1. https://mailchi.mp/081b88e5b445/lcmortimer

Hybrid Academy: Year One

Do you love academy stories full of adventure and magic?
Check out Hybrid Academy: Year One now!! You can also
keep reading for a sneak peek!

"This isn't what I ordered." The tall man in the suit looked at the coffee and sneered. He thrust the cup back at me. A little bit sloshed over the side of the cup and onto the counter. "And you'd better clean that up."

Biting back irritation, I managed a smile.

"Of course. Anything else I can do for you?" I asked politely. Inside, I felt anything but polite. This guy was being a total jerk, as always. I knew for a fact that his coffee had been made perfectly. He just didn't like me because I couldn't do magic.

He wanted Maggie to make his drink.

"A free bagel couldn't hurt," the man said, jerking his head toward the display of blueberry bagels.

"I'll have to get my manager's permission," I said. "Please wait just a moment."

I scurried to the back of the café and knocked on the door to the office.

"Come in."

I yanked the door open and peered inside. Tony was sitting at his desk with his ankles crossed over the top. He looked bored out of his mind.

"What do you want, Maxine?" He asked.

"It's Max," I said. "Not Maxine. And there's a customer who wants a free bagel."

"We don't give out bagels for free," Tony said with a yawn. He was obviously bored. He was always bored at the café.

"I know, but he said that his drink was wrong and he wants to be compensated with free food."

Tony glared at me and got up with a huff. He acted like it was my fault that he was the manager of the café or that he had to leave the safety of his office to come do his actual job. Whatever. I'd been dealing with Tony ever since I started working at the café. He was neither a good boss nor a team player, so I tried to stay as far away from him as possible. Besides, something about Tony made me uncomfortable, and I couldn't quite pinpoint why.

"Is there a problem, Lionel?" Tony asked the tall man.

"Yeah, your em-ploy-ee," he dragged the word out sarcastically. "Messed up my drink. I asked her nicely if she could fix it."

"Not a problem," Tony said. He jerked his head toward one of my coworkers. "Maggie, make Lionel a new drink."

Maggie shot me a nasty look but nodded and started the drink. The café wasn't busy and the drink wasn't complicated, so I wasn't sure what the big deal was. Actually, I had the distinct feeling that Lionel's original drink had been just fine, but that he wanted a bagel out of the deal.

Correction: he wanted a *free* bagel.

Tony and Lionel sat and chatted while Maggie made the drink. I cleaned up the spill on the counter before starting to check our inventory. I wasn't a magic user, so I couldn't just summon cups whenever we ran out of something we needed. Instead, I'd have to trot back to the stockroom, find what we needed, and carry it back. It was kind of a drag for everyone, which was just another reason nobody liked me.

By the time I left work that day, I was tired, exhausted, and spent.

And I knew my grandmother was going to be beyond pissed that I was late.

I RAN UP THE STEPS to the little log cabin where I lived with my Grandmother. My heart was pounding, racing, and I silently begged it to stop. *Slow down.* It needed to chill out, to be honest. Overreacting never turned out well for anyone, least of all me.

I smelled sweaty and I was tired: both signs that I left work much later than I should have. I didn't want her to give me a hard time about it. Mémère had enough to worry about. She didn't need to be concerned that my boss still wasn't letting me leave on time or that my customers were constantly giving me a hard time.

That's the price I paid to work at a café in Brooksville.

Nobody liked me because I was poor, and an orphan, and I couldn't do magic.

All of those elements combined to make me one of the most disliked people in town. Despite trying to have a charming personality and showing kindness to the people around me, I somehow still managed to catch the eye of every magic-user within shouting distance, and not in a good way.

I glanced down at my work clothes. My once-white blouse was now splattered with coffee, no thanks to Maggie and Justine for their "assistance" at work. My jeans had fared just as poorly. They had a few new stains, a new tear, and smelled slightly questionable. I sighed. Mémère was definitely going to notice something was wrong.

I hated to make her worry.

I hated to make her sad.

She worked so hard to raise me, to take care of me, that the idea of letting her down again filled me with stress and anxiety. I wished for the millionth time that I could use magic. I wished that I had a wand, that I knew spells, or that I had, you know, *powers*. I wished that I could whisper a few carefully practiced words and somehow whip up an appearance she could be proud of.

But I couldn't.

In my case, practice hadn't made perfect.

I stared at the front door of our home for a long minute. My breathing finally began to stabilize and I began to feel like everything was going to be okay. Maybe it would. Maybe everything would be fine. One bad day at work wouldn't kill me.

A hundred bad days at work wouldn't kill me.

Besides, I owed Mémère *everything*. Without her, I wouldn't exist. I would have died when my parents did. I would have been killed or lost or starved. No one else in this place was about to take in a little orphan kid who couldn't do spells. Nobody. Yet my grandmother was ready.

My grandmother was brave.

I reached for the door and pressed my hand against it, but I didn't turn the knob. Not yet. I needed a few more minutes to be alone with my thoughts, to focus on the fact that today had been the worst day yet. Today seemed different somehow. Part of me thought that after awhile, things at work would get easier. I thought that they'd improve and that I would finally begin to connect with people who understood me.

I was so wrong.

I'm not understood now, just like I wasn't understood before.

A tear slid down my cheek and I brushed it away. I look around wildly, like someone could see me, even though I was completely alone.

"I know you're out there," I heard her voice through the door. "Come on in, love. I won't bite."

I gulped.

Yeah, my grandmother definitely knew something was up. She didn't want me working in town, anyway, but I had convinced her that I needed to. The reality was that I knew she didn't have a lot of money and I felt bad for not contributing to our family. The café didn't bring in a lot of money, but I was finished with school and wasn't really doing anything else with my time.

There weren't a lot of job prospects in Brookville, but the café was something. It enabled me to make some money, spend time socializing, and get to know people who lived near me. It meant I could be around other people, for once. It meant I could explore the world, if only just a little.

The front door opened before I could turn the knob, and there stood my grandmother: tall, lean, and silvery.

Fierce.

My grandma was fierce.

Everything about her screamed *strong*. She was taller than me, which was sometimes hard for me to grasp since at 5'7", I wasn't a tiny girl. Although she was getting older, she still had strong muscles that were clearly defined. Whether it was from being a witch or from years of exercise and hard work, I wasn't sure. I just knew that my grandma wasn't the type of person anyone messed with.

Not if they knew what was good for them.

"You're late," she said simply, but she glared when she did. Her eyes narrowed a little: not too much. She didn't quite look *mad*. It was more like, a cautious sort of look, as though she was waiting for me to say something first. I knew exactly what she wanted from me. She wanted me to admit that working in the shop was a bad choice and that I was ready to stay home with her.

After all, even if I couldn't use magic, I could still learn about it, and my grandmother loved it when I studied.

"Not by much," I responded, but I knew instantly it was the wrong thing to say. My grandmother didn't yell at me or raise her voice. She never had. We didn't have that kind of relationship. Besides, disappointment was so much worse than yelling, anyway. If I wanted to trick Gram, I should have acted stupid. I should have pretended like I didn't know just how late it was. Then I could have pretended that I was lollygagging or chatting with someone and just completely lost track of the time.

My answer let her know that I knew I was late, and that there was a reason for it.

"What happened?" She said gently. Her eyes softened when she looked at me. Mr. Boo, my familiar, came out of the cabin and rubbed against my legs. I reached down and picked up the fat, black-and-white cat and held him in my arms for a minute. Somehow, Boo always managed to calm my racing heart when I felt stressed. I might not do magic, but Grams had given him to me just the same.

"Every witch should have a familiar," she had told me that day. Boo had been a full-grown cat already. No one knew exactly how old he was or where he'd come from, but Gram had chosen him and he turned out to be just as special as she thought he would.

"It's nothing, Mémère," I told her. "I just got caught up at work."

"Did you get busy at work, Maxine, or did someone make you stay late out of spite?" She didn't ask it in an accusing way, but I knew what she was thinking. Mémère didn't like me working for my boss. She didn't understand why I wanted to work or why I thought it was important that I have a job of some sort.

Any sort.

In her mind, my time would be better spent helping out on the property, working in the yard, or memorizing spells from the big, heavy book she kept on the kitchen table. The pages were worn with years of use, but Grams told me every day how important those spells were.

Not that I'd ever use them.

The little cabin we lived in was surrounded by a wide yard and then trees for as far as the eye could see. Our driveway itself was almost a mile long. That's how hidden away we were. Unless someone was looking for us specifically, they'd never find us. We didn't even get mail at the house. Everything went to a post office box in town that one of us would check on a weekly basis.

Mémère and I were isolated, and she worried about me.

"You know Tony likes to have me stay late sometimes," I finally said. It wasn't a lie, but it was sort of a half-truth. I didn't know if Tony actually liked having me stay or if he just liked having me miserable. Did I get paid for staying late? Yeah. Of course. This wasn't some sort of illegal café. That said, it was still a nightmare working late after I'd already been on my feet for an eight-hour shift.

My grandmother sighed and shook her head.

"This man is no good for you," she said.

"He's not my man," I pointed out. I didn't date. Mémère knew that. A lot of things kept me from relationships and one of the biggest reasons was that I didn't want to date a magic user. It wasn't my thing. I couldn't use magic. I had never been able to get even the simplest spell to work. My grandmother did her best to train me in the ways of her people, but somehow, I'd just never managed to pick things up.

If it bothered her, she was kind enough not to tell me.

Still, I didn't want to date someone who could use magic. Part of it was a safety thing. Self-preservation was important and I didn't want to be in a relationship with someone who might do a love spell on me. I just hated the idea of not knowing what was going on.

I hated the idea that someone might take advantage of me.

"He's still cruel," Mémère said. She shook her head. She was disappointed. In me? In the situation? I wasn't sure, but I nodded in agreement and moved past her and into the house. I dropped my bag on the living room sofa and walked into the attached kitchen. The book with Mémère's spells, as always, was spread out in the center of the table. Gram had been working on spells this afternoon. Herbs and pots and potions and bottles were on every flat surface in the room.

"What were you working on?" I asked her, but she only shook her head gently. Grams never liked to talk about the spells she was doing. I didn't really understand why it had to be a secret. She wanted me to trust her, but there were so many things she wouldn't reveal to me.

"Are you hungry?" Mémère asked, and I knew there was to be no discussion on what she was trying to do with her spell book. It didn't make sense to me. Sometimes it seemed like she had just as many secrets as Mom and Dad.

"I ate at work," I lied. She looked at me carefully. Was she trying to see if I was lying? I totally was, but this time, there was no way for her to tell. Not unless she used some sort of truth serum on me. I wouldn't put it past her, but this wasn't something I was ready to talk about today. Not with Grams.

"If you change your mind..." Her voice trailed off and I nodded.

"Don't worry. I'm 19, Grams. I'm old enough to make myself something to eat."

I kissed her softly on the cheek and turned to the little staircase that led upstairs. Our home was very cozy, but it was also very small. The second floor of the cabin had only two little bedrooms and a tiny bathroom with a sink, a toilet, and a shower. I went up the stairs and sat at the very top for a minute. I listened to see if I could figure out what Gram was up to.

I heard her bustling around in the kitchen for awhile, touching things and whispering, but she was so quiet that I couldn't make out the words. When Boo came up the narrow staircase and rubbed against my legs, I reached for him and pet him softly. Instantly, he started to purr.

"At least I have you," I whispered, and I pulled him into my lap. I held Boo for a long time. Then I stood up and carried him into my bedroom and shut the door behind me. I locked the door. It didn't matter. If Gram needed to come in, she could cast a spell and be in my space in like, two seconds.

But the lock made me feel like I was tucking myself away from everything: my boss, my job, my lack of friends. I used it because it gave me a little bit of security I wouldn't otherwise have. I lay on my bed and looked at the ceiling.

"What am I going to do, Boo?"

He purred and plopped his fat body onto my tummy. I pet him as I looked up at the white popcorn finish on the ceiling. I imagined that I was back home – at my real home – with my mom and dad. They'd been gone for years. Sometimes it felt like forever. I missed them still.

People always said that life got better. They said things like "time heals all wounds" and "one day, it won't hurt so bad," but that wasn't true, was it? Things still hurt. I still missed the way my mom sang songs while she cooked spaghetti and the way my dad laughed as he danced in the kitchen with her. I missed the way they read me bedtime stories and how they used to count the stars with me. I missed everything about them.

Mémère was a wonderful person. She was kind and brave and I was so incredibly lucky to have her, but...

But she wasn't my mom.

And sometimes I just wanted my mom.

Finally, I got up and started getting ready for bed. I went into the bathroom and brushed my teeth and my hair. Then I came back, brushed Boo, and picked out my outfit for the next day. I double checked my work schedule and figured out what time I needed to get up in order to make it in for my shift. Then I closed my eyes.

I tried to fall asleep, but I laid in bed thinking for what seemed like hours.

I heard a crash, and Mémère let out a string of swear words. She would be working late into the night, I guessed, and I had no idea what she was doing down there.

What was so important that she couldn't tell me about it?

And why did I have the feeling it wasn't anything good?

Want to keep reading? Get your copy of Hybrid Academy: Year One now.

Just Another Day in the Zombie Apocalypse

Hey reader! Are you a fan of zombie novels? Adventures? Stories that make you wonder how well *you'd* fare in the apocalypse? Check out the first chapter of *Just Another Day in the Zombie Apocalypse.*

ALICE OPENED HER EYES.

She immediately regretted her decision.

Heat swept over her body. The sun was blaring, and if she had to guess, she was probably burnt. Badly.

Then again, maybe not.

She sat up and looked around, shocked to see billows of smoke surrounding the building.

Fuck.

Was it on fire?

Had she really slept that long?

"Get up," she shook Mark, who had fallen asleep next to her, and tried to wake him up. "Something's wrong," she insisted.

"Yeah," he grumbled, rolling over. "You're waking me up before noon."

Something wasn't right. She stood and walked to the ledge of the apartment building. They had slept on the roof last night after the party. It was just a normal party: nothing crazy, so what was with the sky being so weird? The city wasn't any louder than usual, but the smoke? That was too close to them for her to be comfortable with.

Alice looked out over the city and her heart dropped. She was on the roof of a 12-story building overlooking the city of Holbrook, and from what she could see, the world was in chaos. There were cars parked in the middle of the road, people walking and running, suitcases everywhere. Dropped purses lined the street, along with trash and food.

What the hell was going on?

It must be some sort of national emergency or natural disaster, but what could it be? She couldn't see where the fire was. There had to be a fire. There was so much smoke that surely, there was a fire. She just couldn't see it yet.

"Something is wrong," she repeated, but her voice must have sounded more urgent because this time, Mark opened his eyes and sat up.

"What is it?"

"I think there's a fire. I can't see it."

The two of them moved over to the edge of the roof and peered down into the city.

"What the hell?" Mark muttered. "Was there an earthquake or something?"

"An earthquake that caused a fire? I don't think so."

They watched as a car crashed into a fire hydrant and water burst out, spilling onto the road.

"What happened to the fire department?" Mark asked, echoing Alice's thoughts.

"Better question: what happened to everyone?" They stared at the madness. Helplessness filled Alice's heart as she was stuck watching the insanity from their position on the roof. She tried to fight the growing panic in her chest, but soon she had to admit there was a problem, a serious one, and not one they'd be able to solve while they stood around on the roof.

"We need to go," she said.

"Go where?" A groggy voice said from behind them, and they turned to see Kyle. Alice exchanged knowing glances with Mark. They had both forgotten Kyle was there.

"Something's wrong," Alice said, walking back to him. She took his hand and yanked him to his feet. Kyle was a scrawny kid, maybe about 150 pounds soaking wet, and gangly. He reminded Alice of someone's little brother.

Maybe everyone's little brother.

Kyle lived down the hall from Alice and Mark and he worked as some sort of computer repair guy. Alice wasn't really sure. The only thing she knew about Kyle is that he was awful at drinking games and she had beat him every round last night.

"What is it? Like a drill or something?" Kyle rubbed his eyes and moved to the edge of the roof where Mark was still standing. He peered over and immediately jumped back. "Zombies!" He said.

"Don't be stupid," Mark told him, but Kyle was certain.

"We always knew it was going to happen," Kyle said. "You jocks didn't believe us, but we knew. We always knew." He shook his head back and forth, as if trying to convince himself of the reality, then turned to Alice. "We need to get out of here."

"I don't want to overreact," Alice said hesitantly, but to her surprise, Mark agreed with Kyle.

"I know you're nervous that we're going to think you're a worry wart," he said, not unkindly. "But this is serious, Al. Even if it's not zombies," he rolled his eyes. "It's something. And I don't think we should wait around to see what happens next."

Alice looked once more down at the city, as if staring would make everything change, make everything go back to normal, but she knew as she looked over Holbrook that nothing would be the same again.

Amid the smoke, amid the flames, amid the cars honking and blaring, she suddenly saw something that made her gag, then vomit over the edge of the roof.

"Al, you okay? Al, what is it?" Mark was at her side, rubbing her back. She couldn't stop puking, so she pointed, down into the crowd.

She knew the second Mark saw the Infected eating a person he'd pulled from a car because Mark stopped touching her and said, "Let's go. Let's go *now*."

Somehow, Alice managed to stop throwing up long enough to move her feet. She grabbed her cell phone and slipped her flip-flops on before they headed downstairs.

"Pack a bag," Mark said. "Only essential items. Grab what you need, especially food, if you have it. Meet in the hall in ten."

"Got it," Kyle said, and scurried down the stairs to the top floor of the apartment building. "Watch out, guys. Power's out," he called back up.

Alice looked at Mark and back down the stairs. Was she ready to descend into the darkness? She wasn't sure. This was *so* not how she had planned to spend her weekend. Had she wanted to drink? Yes. Had she wanted to party? A little. But zombies? Not so much.

If they even were zombies, that is, because in reality, who really knew? Kyle was just a geek with an overactive imagination. What did he even know about chaos in the world? Maybe there really *had* been an earthquake or a tornado or something completely natural that could be conquered with a bit of time, patience, and help from the National Guard. Maybe there was a perfectly logical explanation for what she *thought* she'd seen looking down on the town.

There had to be.

"Alice," Mark nudged her. "Come on. It's going to be fine, okay? I promise."

She nodded. She could do this. She stepped carefully down the stairs, clutching the rail with one hand and holding her phone up as a light in the other. This floor was supposed to be used for storage, so it was abandoned and quiet. People rarely wandered up to the 12th floor unless they wanted to put their coats away for the winter.

Alice got off the stairs and saw Kyle waiting patiently nearby. Mark followed her quickly down the stairs, then they went together down to the 11th floor where their apartments were.

"I'll meet you back here in five," Kyle said, popping into his apartment.

"Ditto," Mark said. He turned to Alice. "You going to be okay?"

"Yeah," she said. "I'm fine."

She went to her apartment and fished her keys from her pocket, then unlocked the door. It was weird to see it so dark in the daytime and her hand automatically flicked the lights on.

Nothing.

"Come on, Alice," she said out loud. "You can do this." Her voice sounded strange in the darkness: forced, almost. She felt like she was doing something she wasn't supposed to be, like she was being sneaky somehow. She knew it was stupid, that she was being silly, but she couldn't quite knock the notion out of her head.

Alice quickly crossed her tiny living room and opened the blinds to let some light into the room. Unfortunately, the natural light streaming in picked up on all the dust she had floating around her apartment. Gross. She really needed to be better at cleaning, but she was always so busy at work that she just didn't put that much effort in at home. Now it showed.

Alice kicked off her flip-flops. Then she grabbed her backpack from the kitchen counter and emptied out her library books. She had been planning on reading this weekend for work in preparation for a case they had coming up at the legal office where she worked, but that obviously wasn't going to happen.

Even if this was just a misunderstanding, as she hoped it was, or some sort of weird natural disaster, Alice wouldn't be going to work this week. A feeling of dread settled in the pit of her stomach as she wondered what the hell had happened last night.

Was she *that* drunk that she didn't hear anything?

Granted, she didn't usually drink. Not much, anyway. She'd been a lightweight in college and even now as a recent graduate, she tended to stick with soda over beer.

But last night had been about relaxing, unwinding. It had been a long week and her boss had been awful and she just wanted some time to herself.

Was that really so bad?

She opened her fridge and pulled out a couple of water bottles. Alice shoved them in her backpack, along with a jar of nuts and a bag of beef jerky. In her bedroom, she grabbed a clean set of clothes and looked longingly toward her bathroom. She wanted a shower. She felt gross. Maybe there was time for one.

Just as she was debating whether or not to take a quick rinse, her door flew open and Mark and Kyle bolted in.

"We have to go," Mark said. "Now."

"Okay," Alice said, starting toward them. She stopped and turned, taking one last look at her apartment. Was she forgetting anything? She had packed so quickly. Maybe she was forgetting something.

"No, like *now*," Kyle grabbed her hand and yanked her into the hall. Mark grabbed her backpack and a pair of shoes. He closed the door behind them and shoved the shoes at Alice.

"Wanna tell me what's going on?" She asked, slipping her feet into them, trying her best not to fall over and embarrass herself.

Kyle and Mark exchanged looks, but Alice rolled her eyes.

"Not the time to play coy, boys," she said.

"It's zombies," Kyle said. "I know it. And they're already in the building, and we need to get out."

"Do you own a gun?" Mark asked, and Alice shook her head. She'd never seen the need for one. Her father had been quite the gun nut, but her? She just wanted to make a name for herself. She didn't get all caught up in politics and gun rights or anything like that. It had never interested her, so she hadn't taken the time to buy a gun.

Now she felt like an idiot.

"No," she admitted.

"Kyle's got one. I have this," Mark held up a bat she hadn't noticed. "But we need to go. Now. You stay behind us. Don't let anything bite you or, you know, bleed on you."

It all felt surreal. There was no way this could be happening, yet as the men led her to the stairwell, she realized that it definitely, absolutely, was happening.

"We'll go to your car," Kyle whispered. "If we get separated, meet up there and we'll all go together, okay?"

"Got it."

Mark opened the door to the stairwell that separated the stairs from the hallway. It was empty. They quickly darted down the stairs. Alice didn't have to ask how the guys knew there were zombies. She could hear the cries from each floor as they passed one after the other. They didn't slow down, didn't stop to help, didn't try to peek to confirm their suspicions.

They'd all seen enough horror movies to know better.

And now, now Alice had to make it to the car. Her Hyundai wasn't the world's best vehicle, but it had been a gift to herself when she landed her job at Smith & McArthur. The legal firm was known for being highly selective in its employees, and she had celebrated by buying herself a new car.

She had taken out a loan, of course, which her parents thought was irresponsible, but she had been happy with her decision.

Until now.

Now she wished she had splurged even more on a Humvee. Or a tank.

They passed each floor and the cries grew louder and more dramatic. She heard a few gunshots and realized some of her neighbors were fighting back. On the 5th floor, there was blood smeared across the window that led to the interior hallway.

On the 4th floor, she could see a snarling, angry person covered in blood. Was it Infected?

On the 3rd floor, the door was completely ripped off its hinges and the remnants of a battle were splayed across the stairs and railings.

"Be careful," Kyle warned. "Don't touch the blood."

"I thought you could only turn if you got bitten by a zombie," Alice said. Maybe her horror trivia was a bit rusty.

"We don't know how it spreads," Mark said calmly. "So just keep your hands to yourself and keep moving." He gripped the bat in his hands and followed her down the stairs. The floor was slippery and once she grabbed the railing to steady herself, barely missing a bloody spot on the rail. Luckily, neither of the guys saw it.

She didn't want them to go full-on zombie-movie mode where they murdered her just for getting blood on her. When they reached the first floor, they stopped and peeked through the clear window that led to the lobby.

Furniture was strewn about and there was a body in the center of the floor. Just one.

"Ken," Alice whispered, but Mark clamped a hand over her mouth and pointed. There was an Infected in the corner. It was near the body, but no longer chomping on what used to be Ken. Covered in blood, the creature, or zombie, or whatever it should be called, was looking at Ken.

It wiped its mouth with the back of its hand, as if satisfied after a meal.

Then it looked up.

It looked straight toward them and immediately started charging the door.

"Parking lot!" Mark called, and they hurried through the door behind the stairs that led to the parking lot. They heard a loud thud as the creature threw its body at the door again and again. "Move!"

Alice focused on her car and yanked the keys from her pocket. The car was in the first row, luckily, and only about 20 feet from the door. She hurried and unlocked the driver's side door, then hit the locks for the rest of the car. Mark and Kyle both piled in the backseat with their bags and weapons.

"Go!" Kyle said. "Let's hit it, Alice."

She started the engine and began to drive. She knew the main road by their apartment complex was trashed, so she took the back parking lot exit that led to a side road. Hopefully that one would be a little more clear.

Hopefully that one would offer some sort of escape.

Hopefully they weren't all about to die.

ALICE PEELED OUT OF the parking lot and cringed at the squeal of her tires. She had lived in Holbrook for all of a year, ever since she graduated from college, and she hated how expensive it was to live there. Everything cost money and even now, even with the world around her falling apart, all she could think about was how much it was going to cost to fix her tires if she messed them up.

Mark hollered directions from the backseat and Alice did her best to follow them. Her ex-military neighbor was smart and attentive. She probably should have let him drive, but somehow, Mark seemed comfortable in the back, looking out the windows. He was watching everything, she realized, taking it all in.

Mark had spent a year overseas. Maybe more. She knew it was at least a year. Afghanistan, maybe. Alice wasn't really sure. What she did know was that Mark was ready for anything, even if he didn't own his own gun. She could see the wheels in his mind turning, formulating some sort of plan.

What was going to happen to them?

She could see from the road that they hadn't wasted any time leaving town. Bodies were piling up. On the side road she had taken, people were running around screaming, trying to load up their cars, and sitting on their roofs.

"That's not going to help them," Kyle commented. "They'll get dehydrated and die anyway, or they'll starve. That's the worst place they could go."

"They're scared," Alice said. "They don't know what to do."

"Rule number one of a crisis situation is 'don't panic,'" Mark told them. "They might not know what to do, but they're definitely panicking. Kyle is right. You can't go sit on the roof and hope the zombies will somehow decide to go away. They aren't going away. This isn't some fictional story with a happy ending."

Alice turned down another road and slammed on the brakes immediately, but she wasn't fast enough. She slammed into a stopped car ahead of her and groaned as her chest hit the seatbelt. She heard Mark and Kyle muttering curses from the back of the car, but then they both started yelling at her to get out of the car and run.

That was when she saw it.

Alice lifted her eyes and looked ahead at the horde approaching from ahead of her.

That's what it was: a horde. There was no other word for it. Zombies upon zombies were walking down the road, making their way around cars and bodies, and they were all headed straight for the trio.

One word echoed in her head.

Run.

Just Another Day in the Zombie Apocalypse is now available for purchase. Get your copy today!

Don't miss out!

Visit the website below and you can sign up to receive emails whenever L.C. Mortimer publishes a new book. There's no charge and no obligation.

https://books2read.com/r/B-A-XYLC-QTIJB

BOOKS 2 READ

Connecting independent readers to independent writers.

Also by L.C. Mortimer

Enchanted Academy
The Wolf
The Fairy
The Hook
Enchanted Academy Box Set: The Complete Collection Books
1-4
The Beauty

Which Village
A Hex A Day

Standalone
Swords of Darkness
Just Another Day in the Zombie Apocalypse: Episode 1
The Lost Fallen
Outbreak: A Zombie Novel
Shifter Falls Academy: Year Two

Beyond Rainbows: A Zombie Novel
Blood Rum: A Vampire Story
She Smiles at Midnight
Spunky

Made in the USA
Columbia, SC
10 September 2024

41444126R00104